"You Sleep Around Quite a Bit," He Murmured. "Don't You?"

"Do I?" Charley held Brant's penetrating gaze with admirable steadiness, considering the turmoil his question had created in her. She felt stuck in a mold of her own design. She couldn't very well deny the reputation she herself had created.

"Would you consider sleeping with me?"

Check! This time the flutter of Charley's mascaraed lashes was without artifice. With six softly muttered words Brant had succeeded where many before him had failed.

JOAN HOHL
is a Gemini and an inveterate daydreamer and says that she always had her head in the clouds. Though she reads eight or nine books a week, she only discovered Romances ten years ago. "But as soon as I read the first one," she confesses, "I was hooked." Now an extremely popular author, she is thrilled to be getting paid for exactly what she loves doing best. Joan Hohl also writes under the pseudonym of Amii Lorin.

Dear Reader:

I'd like to take this opportunity to thank you for all your support and encouragement of Silhouette Romances.

Many of you write in regularly, telling us what you like best about Silhouette, which authors are your favorites. This is a tremendous help to us as we strive to publish the best contemporary romances possible.

All the romances from Silhouette Books are for you, so enjoy this book and the many stories to come.

Karen Solem
Editor-in-Chief
Silhouette Books

JOAN HOHL
A Taste for Rich Things

Silhouette *Romance*

Published by Silhouette Books New York

America's Publisher of Contemporary Romance

Silhouette Books by Joan Hohl

Thorne's Way (SE #54)
Moments Harsh, Moments Gentle (IM #35)
A Taste for Rich Things (ROM #334)

SILHOUETTE BOOKS, a Division of Simon & Schuster, Inc.
1230 Avenue of the Americas, New York, N.Y. 10020

Distributed by Pocket Books

ISBN: 0-671-57334-9

First Silhouette Books printing January, 1985

10 9 8 7 6 5 4 3 2 1

Map by Ray Lundgren

America's Publisher of Contemporary Romance

Printed in the U.S.A.

To Gayle Link
with thanks
for her encouragement and humor
during the execution of the work.
But most of all for
her friendship.

A Taste for
Rich Things

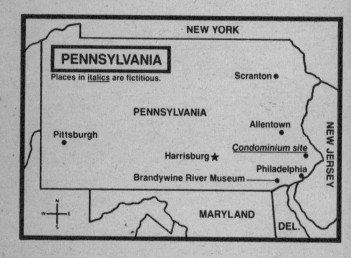

PENNSYLVANIA

Places in _italics_ are fictitious.

NEW YORK

Scranton

PENNSYLVANIA

NEW JERSEY

Pittsburgh

Allentown

Condominium site

Harrisburg ★

Philadelphia

Brandywine River Museum

MARYLAND

DEL.

Chapter One

"I want that man."

Charlott Marks, her gaze fastened on the male in question, was hardly aware of the gasp that burst from the woman seated beside her.

"Charley, really, someone might hear you!"

Charlott's stare remained riveted on the tall man standing at the edge of the dance floor. Lord, he certainly was something to look at! Charlott unconsciously slid the tip of her tongue over her bottom lip. He had to be six four if he was an inch! And every one of those inches was covered with dark coppery skin.

"That really worries me," she finally responded dryly. Distractedly, Charlott lifted her glass and sipped at the very expensive champagne it contained. She didn't even taste the cool liquid. "Do you have any idea who he is?" Reluctantly, Charlott wrenched her eyes away from the stranger's tall form to gaze quizzically at her friend.

"No." Gayle Peters, Charlott's closest friend, gave
the man a quick glance and shuddered delicately. "And
I'm not sure I'd want to. For all the elegant draping, he
looks like a tough customer to me." Gayle's soft brown
eyes held a hint of apprehension. She knew her friend;
once Charley decided on a course of action, she pursued
it relentlessly. Her apprehension grew at the smile that
curved Charley's perfectly shaped lips.

"Yes, he does, doesn't he?" Charlott laughed softly,
amused by Gayle's expression and her observation. "An
excitingly tough customer. Have you ever in your life
seen a profile like that?" Charley's smile widened to
reveal even white teeth. "Puts me in mind of a hatchet
blade." Her clear blue eyes dancing with amusement,
Charley smothered her laughter as she watched Gayle's
head swivel in the man's direction. Her own gaze again
sought the striking male visage.

The tall man's profile was indeed sharply delineated.
His head was capped by thick, straight, silky looking
black hair, a trifle long at his nape. It gleamed with near
blue highlights in the light from the huge chandeliers
overhead. His wide forehead was accentuated by a swath
of black that persisted in falling out of place. Black
eyebrows, not bushy, not thin, arched defiantly over
deep-set dark eyes. His nose was also arched, and long,
giving the impression of aristocratic arrogance. His lips
were thin, harshly defined. His cheekbones were high,
his jawline square, both aggressively jutting and in
perfect symmetry with his nose.

He was dressed in much the same fashion as all the
other men in the large ballroom, yet the black evening
garb and white ruffled shirt pointed out the difference

between him and them. With few exceptions, the other men looked like uncomfortable penguins. The tall man, however, was obviously not intimidated by the formal attire.

His head turned in response to a remark from a man in front of him, affording Charley her first full view of his face. He was harshly handsome in a way that might frighten most women. Gayle's assessment was correct; he looked tough . . . and powerful, and more than a little fierce. He also looked sexy as hell!

Charlott Marks was not like most women. She was not at all frightened by his aura of masculine power or by his fierce looks. Quite the contrary; Charley was intrigued, gripped with a nervous excitement unlike anything she'd ever experienced before. Her own words of a few minutes before, murmured without conscious thought, became conviction as she stared at him. She *wanted* that man!

"Charley, I know that expression." Gayle's soft tone did little to mask her growing concern. "Every time you get that look of grim determination, it means trouble, or scandal, or both!" Gayle's expressive brown eyes revealed her fear. "The gossip has barely died down from your last escapade. Please, please, don't do anything foolish."

Charley's elegantly winged auburn brows rose disdainfully. "Are you suggesting I have a reputation?" Bringing the stemmed glass to her lips, she sipped daintily. "Me?" Long mascara-darkened lashes fluttered over crystal blue eyes that were wide with innocence. "I am completely crushed." A soft, heartfelt sigh punctuated her assertion.

"You are completely mad!" Gayle exclaimed, eyeing Charley fearfully. "Why do you do the outrageous things you do?"

Blue eyes teased Gayle over the rim of the fragile glass. "Because life is so utterly boring when you play by the rules." Without moving her head, Charley slid her glance over the tall, formally clad figure. "I'd bet he doesn't play by the rules either." One long blood-red fingernail tapped the glass lightly. "What do you suppose he is, Gayle?" she mused aloud. "Spanish? French, perhaps?"

"Trouble."

"Undoubtedly!" Charley's soft, enchanting laughter wafted on the air in the crowded room, drawing appreciative smiles from the occupants seated at the tables closest to hers. "Trouble spiced with excitement! Long cold nights between hot steamy sheets." This assertion drew a louder gasp from her shocked friend.

"I don't know why anything you say still surprises me, but it does!" Gayle's tone conveyed a long-suffering note. "Nor do I understand why you should choose to wear the cloak of promiscuity. You are the most fastidious person I have ever known."

"Lower your voice!" Charley exclaimed in a whisper, glancing around quickly. "Are you trying to clean up the name I've worked so hard to tarnish?" Charley's smile was full of mischief. "But, back to that gorgeous male animal across the room. I wasn't trying to shock you, Gayle. I felt all kinds of tingles the moment I spied him standing head and shoulders above the men surrounding him. Now"—Charley bit her lip in concentration—"help me figure out a way of getting his attention."

"Stand up."

"What?"

"Charley, all you have to do is stand up," Gayle said patiently. "If the man is human, he'll notice you." Gayle slowly surveyed Charley from head to waist. "You are the most ravishing woman in this room." A teasing smile curved Gayle's lips. "And you know it as well as I do."

Charley fought hard to contain a grin. "There are lots of beautiful women here tonight," she observed.

"True." Gayle nodded seriously. "Beautiful, but not ravishing. Let's call it as it is. You see the same thing in your mirror as I see when I look at you." Gayle was long past being overwhelmed by Charlott's exceptional beauty. Now she held up one small hand, ticking off Charley's attributes on her plump fingers. "First of all, your face alone could intimidate any beauty." At Charley's gurgle of laughter, Gayle's tone turned scolding. "Darn it, Charley, it's true, and you know it! Your bone structure is nearly perfect, and with your rosy coloring, the overall effect is gorgeous. The fact that you're five feet eight inches tall and as angularly skinny as a high-fashion model doesn't hurt any either." Her eyes reflecting the amusement dancing in Charley's, Gayle sighed dramatically. "Then, of course, there's that mahogany mop of yours! All things considered," Gayle groaned, "I'm amazed I don't hate the ground you walk on!"

Once again Charley's laughter mingled with the muted roar of conversation in the large room. "Oh, Gayle, you're a real card." With some effort Charley controlled her amusement. "By the time you're fifty-two, you might even be playing with a full deck." She waved one long, slim-fingered hand languidly. "My looks and figure are due to a quirk of nature.'' She tapped her temple with a blood-red fingernail. ''But you know as well as I that it's what's inside here that counts.''

''And you have plenty going for you up there,'' Gayle inserted forcefully. ''That's why I can't understand or accept this devil-may-care image you've created.''

''Tut-tut, counselor.'' Charley arched one delicate auburn brow quellingly. ''I have never presumed to question your choice of profession and, merely because you happen to be my lawyer, please don't presume to question mine.'' Though her tone was light, Charley's voice held an unmistakable thread of steel.

''But that's just it!'' Gayle chose to ignore the warning in her friend's tone. ''You are so very talented, yet you treat your profession as if it were no more than a hobby. I simply do not understand what you are trying to prove with this . . . this . . . vendetta! Damn it, Charley!'' Gayle's curse was a clear indication of her concern; Gayle rarely cursed. ''Why do you hide your true abilities beneath these outrageous escapades?''

''Ah, but that's the whole point, little one.'' Charley's endearment referred to Gayle's size, not her age; in years, Gayle was the senior of the two. ''The only way I can protect myself from society is to appear to be part of it. My escapades, as you call them, amuse me, but they also insulate me.''

Gayle's frustration was made evident by a soft snort. ''Oh, sure, I know all about the way you amuse yourself. If you wish to swim in the nude at a very elegant party at the country estate of a staid society matron, you do it! If you wish to be escorted to a glittering society affair by a rather sinister-looking member of the underworld, you do it! If you wish to drive that outrageously expensive, ridiculously powerful sports car of yours at ninety miles an hour, you do it! And, worst of all, if you choose to get your name in the gossip columns by appearing to be romantically involved with not one, but six different men at the same time, you do it!'' Gayle shook her head as if unable to believe the truth of her accusations, even though she knew too well how very true they all were. ''And all the time, *I* know that you're completely innocent. I swear, Charlott Marks, I simply do not understand what you are trying to prove.''

''I know.'' Charley's smile was briefly shadowed by sadness. ''But, though I'm still innocent, I'm no longer naive. My experiences with high society cured me of that long ago.'' The smile that always set off warning bells in Gayle's mind reappeared on Charley's lips. ''But enough seriousness.'' Her eyes shifted to the tall man across the room. ''Tonight should be more exciting than I dared hope!''

''Charley! You aren't really going to approach that tough-looking giant, are you?'' Gayle groaned. ''Not here, at a reception honoring your father, of all places?''

''Here, there.'' Charley shrugged. ''Makes no difference to me.'' Turning her head, she scanned the room with bright blue eyes. Damned hypocrites, she thought bitterly. For twenty years they ridiculed Dad; now they practically trample each other in the rush to get to him with their fawning praise. Tipping the glass to her lips, Charley gulped down her wine in an effort to wash away the acrid taste in her mouth. How she despised all these people! Charley's roaming gaze came to an abrupt halt on the tall, copper-skinned man. You are beautiful, mister, but you're probably every bit as despicable as the rest of these posturing monkeys, she thought nastily.

At that moment a cherished figure entered Charley's line of vision. Her eyes softened as she watched her father, Stephen Marks, the man of this particular moment, extend his hand to the tall man. Her gaze intent, Charley observed the friendly smile on her father's face. She shifted her glance to catch the other man's reaction. The slash of white teeth in the copper face trapped the breath in Charley's throat. Despicable or not, he was a hunk, and she had to meet him! The decision made, Charley rose gracefully to her feet. It may be the middle of June, tall man, but, prepare yourself, you are about to be taken for a sleigh ride!

"Charley?" Gayle's voice was a comic mixture of warning and entreaty. "What are you going to do?"

Lips twitching with amusement, Charley tilted her head to gaze affectionately at her one true friend. "Relax, little one, I'm merely joining the throng in congratulating my father on his latest invention." Catching sight of a passing waiter, she scooped a glass of champagne from his tray. "Why don't you get up and mix with the elite?" she teased as she strolled off in the direction of her quarry. Her gaze locked on the dark-haired giant, Charley ignored Gayle's sighed "Please remember you are a lady."

A lady indeed! Charley sipped her wine as she glanced at the women standing around her. If these pillars of society are ladies, thank heaven I am not! And thank heaven for the role model I do have! A smile warmed her eyes as a visual image of her father's housekeeper formed in her mind. Big, blunt, and without a false bone in her body, Darlene Holt, the woman Stephen Marks had hired as housekeeper a scant two years before, had become both friend and confidante to Charley, and indispensable to Stephen. Again sipping delicately, Charley slid a glance over the female guests. I would much rather be a real woman like Darlene, she mused, than a so-called "lady."

Charley's plan of action regarding the tall man was simple; she had none. She didn't have any idea of how she'd proceed with his seduction, but seduce him she would! Her eyes beginning to sparkle like sunshine bouncing off crystal, Charley sauntered into the all-male group that included her father and her target. Gliding to a stop beside her father, she slid her arm around his waist.

"Ah, here's my firebrand." Stephen's voice was rich with pride. "Are you enjoying yourself, skinny?" he inquired teasingly, knowing full well that Charley did her best to enjoy herself wherever she happened to be.

Charley would have given the sharp side of her tongue to anyone else with the temerity to call her skinny. From Stephen, the nickname was an endearment. Smiling adoringly into her father's blunt-featured face, Charley tightened her arm in a brief hug. "The dinner was delicious. Your acceptance speech held a proper note of humility." Charley grinned at Stephen's frown of warning—he knew very well how she felt about the honor he'd been awarded. "And now I'm looking for a dancing partner," she finished brightly, deliberately avoiding the tall stranger's eyes.

Stephen's groan was predictable, and exactly what Charley was hoping for. He hated to dance. "Ah, honey . . . I really have a lot of people to talk to, and . . . ah . . ."

"I'd be delighted to stand in for you, sir. If the young

lady wouldn't mind?'' The voice was as dark and smooth as his skin, and every bit as exciting. ''I promise I'll do my best not to stomp on her toes . . . too often.''

''Oh, Brant! I am sorry.'' Stephen smiled apologetically at the younger man. ''Have you met my daughter?''

Very slowly Charley lifted her head to stare into eyes as black as any unrepentant sinner's soul. The impact was immediate and violent. Forbidding herself a shiver of appreciation, Charley extended her right hand as her father made the introduction.

''Charlott, I'd like you to meet Brant d'Acier. Brant, my daughter, Charlott, whom everybody calls Charley.'' An impish grin played at his lips. ''Hardly looks like a Charley, does she?''

A Frenchman, I knew it! Pleased with herself for guessing correctly, Charley smiled brilliantly. ''Mr. d'Acier,'' she murmured throatily. Her hand, not small by any stretch of the imagination, was completely lost inside Brant's much larger one. Her reaction to his warm touch was as violent as it had been to his eyes; this time Charley could not deny the shiver that feathered her naked shoulders and arms.

''A pleasure, Ms. Marks.'' Brant did not actually smile, unless one counted the tiny tilt at the corners of his thin, hard-looking lips. Come to that, Charley mused, he didn't sound all that pleased either! ''May I escort you onto the dance floor?'' he asked politely just as the four-piece combo began playing a current ballad.

Charley laughed softly. ''Is your timing always this good?'' As she posed the question she flickered her lashes with practiced perfection. Her artistry was not

lost on Brant d'Acier. Black brows with the devil's own
natural arch rose in return.

"Always," Brant assured her dryly before glancing at
her father. "And I agree with you, sir," he added.
"Charlott hardly looks like a Charley."

Stephen's laughter followed Charley as she preceded
Brant onto the dance floor. When Brant encircled her
waist with his arms, Charley was left with little choice
but to raise her hands to his shoulders. Cautioning
herself against moving too swiftly, she laid her palms
lightly on the fine black material that enhanced the
breadth of his chest. Her attempt to maintain some
distance between them was met by a glance of amusement from her partner.

"So, you are the famous Charley Marks." Brant
deliberately drawled the remark. He had been hearing of
and reading about Charlott Marks for some months now.
Very little of what he'd heard or read had been good.
With cool disdain Brant had dismissed Stephen's daughter as a trampy madcap, indulging herself with her
father's newfound wealth. Now, having met Charley,
Brant's opinion of her was unchanged. Yet he found
himself powerfully drawn to this infamous siren he was
holding in his eager arms. The sweep of her long lashes
caused a near painful curl of excitement in Brant's loins
that was shocking in its intensity. Bewildered by his own
reaction, Brant stared at Charley out of a face set into
lines of fierce rejection.

Until this moment Charley would have sworn she'd
received, at one time or another, every type of possible
response from the opposite sex. Facing Brant's scowl
with hard-won composure, she speculated on the reason

for his antipathy toward her. Had she appeared too eager to be held in his arms?

"Famous?" Charley did not have to feign the breathless quality in her voice; in fact she was holding her breath. Was it possible that Brant had somehow learned the truth about her—the real truth? A silent sigh of relief whispered through her lips when he clarified himself.

"Your name has appeared in print lately with boring regularity." His voice lowered to a barely perceptible murmur. "You sleep around quite a bit." He ignored Charley's soft gasp as if he hadn't heard it. "Don't you?"

"Do I?" Charley held Brant's penetrating gaze with admirable steadiness. She was at a loss as to how to respond to him. She couldn't very well deny the reputation she herself had created. It really didn't matter, for Brant stole the initiative, and what little breath she had left. Drawing her closer to his hard frame by the simple method of tightening his arms, he proceeded to do what Charley would have insisted was damn near impossible —Brant shocked her to the core.

"Would you consider sleeping with me?"

This time the flutter of Charley's lashes was without artifice. With six softly uttered words Brant had succeeded where many before him had failed: Brant d'Acier had brought Charley to a full mental stop! A rising bubble of laughter threatened to choke her. Who was seducing whom here? Oh, what a pity you are one of the despicable ones, she told him silently, for I think I could really like you! You, sir, are decidedly not a rule abider!

"Really, Mr. d'Acier, I hardly know you!" The shocked astonishment of Charley's tone was as patently false as the innocence of her wide-eyed stare.

"But," he countered softly, "you would know me a lot better after we'd slept together." Again his arms tightened, bringing Charley's entire body into contact with his. This time her gasp elicited a flash of white teeth in a wickedly enticing grin. "Oh, yes, flame top, you would know me one hell of a lot better."

The sexual awareness that Charley had felt at the sight of him shattered into millions of tiny fragments that stabbed at her every erogenous zone. Where? When? Here? Now? Oh, please! The urgency of her own flashing thoughts startled Charley out of the sweetly hot sensuous haze Brant had so effortlessly evoked in her.

Good grief! We are in a crowded ballroom, on an even more crowded dance floor . . . and we're not even dancing! Unless you can call the slow, suggestive movements of our bodies dancing! It wouldn't be entirely incorrect to label the motion lovemaking while fully clothed!

As if in tune with her thoughts, Brant gently thrust his hips into hers. "Say yes, Ms. Marks, and I'll have you out of this crush of babbling idiots and into my quiet bedroom before you know what hit you." Lowering his head, Brant brushed her lips with his own. "Come." His tongue flicked out to stroke Charley's lip. "You've tried the rest, now try the best."

Brant's teasing invitation sent a cold shudder through Charley's body. You've tried the rest. The cool certainty of Brant's statement echoed inside her mind. You've tried the rest. Good heavens! He actually believed everything he had read and heard of her and yet he still wanted her! What kind of man was he?

"I don't think so, Mr. d'Acier." Charley's smile was icy. "Now, if you don't mind?" She pressed her palms against his shoulders to indicate her wish to be set free. "You are crushing my gown." Not to mention my self-image!

"But I do mind," Brant protested softly, astonished at the enormity of the disappointment he felt. God, man! Are you crazy? Brant chastized himself scathingly. This woman has been tossed in the hay more often than a pitchfork! If you have any sense at all, you'll send her on her round-heeled way! Ignoring his own advice, Brant fastened his mouth to the blood-red lure of Charley's slightly parted lips. This was one form of communication that was immediate and direct. Brant groaned involuntarily as sensation after sensation hit the lower part of his body. Reacting without conscious thought, Brant plunged his tongue into the sweetness of Charley's mouth, swelling with triumph at the reciprocal moan that vibrated in her throat. Sanity returned when she tore her lips from the pressure of his. But it was sanity weakened by a passion he had never before experienced. I don't care if she has had a thousand lovers, Brant decided. I must have this woman!

"Mr. d'Acier, please! Remember where we are!"

Charley's gasped protest pierced the sensual haze fogging Brant's usually clear mind. What was happening to him? He never lost control of any situation, most especially one involving a woman! Exerting his considerable willpower, Brant withdrew, physically, emotionally, and mentally from the bright flame of temptation represented by Charley Marks. "Of course." Dropping his arms to his sides, Brant stepped back. Clarity of thought reinstated itself as the distance between them grew to several inches. Brant raked a glance over

Charley's ultraslim frame. "There'll be another time," he promised huskily. "And another, more private place." Damn, she did border on skinny! "And there will be no crushable gown between us." The tip of her tongue left a wet sheen on Charley's lips, and a dry ache in Brant's throat. Oh, sweet Lord! You had better put some distance between yourself and this skinny dame, d'Acier, before the last of your glue becomes unstuck, and you make an absolute ass of yourself. Turning slightly, Brant grasped Charley's arm gently and ushered her off the dance floor. The feel of her warm skin against his palm was nearly Brant's undoing. As he returned Charley to her beaming father, he allowed his hand the freedom of caressing the smooth skin of her upper arm. "Does velvet skin crush?" Brant delivered his parting shot as they came to a halt on the fringes of a group of men effusively congratulating Stephen Marks.

"Only if it's misused."

Brant chuckled in appreciation of Charley's hissed retort. There may not be a hell of a lot to her, he mused, but what there is is held together by sheer courage. No question, this woman will be mine. At least, until I've tested the full measure of her courage.

"There is only one way to use velvet," Brant countered in a drawling whisper. "And that is to burrow into it for warmth."

At a loss for words, Charley glared after Brant's broad-shouldered, narrow-hipped back as he sauntered away from her. Delicious! Charley couldn't pretend she had not understood Brant's final little sexual barb. *She* was the warmth he wanted to burrow into! That man was a walking, talking incitement to riot! Feminine riot! A small, secret smile curved Charley's lips as she swung around to face her father. That big man is riding for a very hard fall, she vowed, dazzling her father's well-wishers with the brilliance of her smile.

"Has Brant cried Uncle already?" Stephen asked with a grin.

Not yet, but I'm sure it won't take long, Charley thought, but all she said was, "I suppose so. I guess you older folk just can't keep pace with the younger set," she teased.

"Older folk!" Stephen's deep-throated laughter erupted with the force of a booming cannon. "Brant would just love that! The man's only thirty-six years old, Charley. Hardly one of the 'older' folk."

"Really?" Though Charley arched her brows disbe-lievingly, mentally she was congratulating herself. Thirty-six was exactly the age she had guessed Brant to be. "I thought he was much older—more your age."

"Did I hear my son's name mentioned in vain?"

Charley's eyes shifted in the direction of the smooth, cultured voice. The black elegance of the man's attire was nothing in comparison to his aristocratically hand-some face and form. Now here, Charley decided, was what a real gentleman looked like. That the man was obviously Brant's father didn't surprise her in the least. Quite the opposite, she could have predicted it.

"I'm afraid so, Louis." Stephen's gleaming eyes belied his somber tone. "But then, my daughter fearless-ly takes any man's name in vain." His grimace was genuine. "Even that of her maker."

"Assuming, of course, that my maker is male," Charley murmured sweetly. "How do you do, sir?" Charley extended her hand with unconscious grace.

"I'm Charlott Marks. I have just had the pleasure of dancing with your son."

"Your servant, Ms. Marks." Louis d'Acier raised Charley's fingers to his lips with old-world courtesy. "And I am Louis d'Acier." Tilting his head, Louis smiled at her out of laughing brown eyes. "Am I mistaken, or were you slighting my son's ability as a dancing partner?"

"It was not your son's finesse on the floor that I was questioning, sir," Charley corrected gently. "It was his staying power." Though her face remained composed, Charley's eyes sparkled with appreciation of their verbal game.

"Surely the cad did not desert you?" Louis asked with exaggerated formality.

"I'm afraid so, sir." Charley sighed in a Victorian manner, then ruined the effect by grinning. "Directly after I refused to share his bed."

"Serves him right." Louis laughed in delight. "Arrogant whelp! Brant's overdue a comeuppance. He's grown much too blasé over the women who so readily fall into his bed."

Indeed! Charley felt a stab of annoyance. Blasé, is he? Women panting all over the place for him, are they? Cancel the sleigh. Bring out the roller coaster. The ride's going to be a wild one! Her father's *harumph* drew Charley out of her thoughts.

"Brant propositioned you?"

Her smile soft with love, Charley raised her hand to caress his cheek with her palm. "Don't let it throw you, darling. I've been propositioned before."

"Not, I hope, by a man working for me!" Stephen sputtered.

"Now, Stephen, I'm sure Brant meant no harm by—" That was as far as Louis got before Charley cut him off.

"Working for you?"

"Yes, working for me, damn it!" Stephen growled. "At least he was working for me when he arrived here this evening."

"Stephen, be reasonable," Louis tried again, only to be interrupted by Charley once more.

"In what capacity does Brant work for you?" Charley knew Stephen's employees very well, all two of them.

"Oh, hell," Stephen groaned. "It was supposed to be a surprise."

"That Brant worked for you?" Charley frowned in confusion.

Stephen's expression turned sour. "No, of course not that he worked for me!" He shrugged in resignation. "I'm having a house built in the suburbs. . . ."

"A house!" Louis inserted indignantly. "A country estate."

"Oh, all right. A country estate!" Stephen snapped. "It was supposed to be a surprise for you, Charlott. Louis, I could strangle that son of yours!"

"Unadvisable." Louis cautioned. "That half-breed of mine would probably take your scalp."

Half-breed? Now Charley was thoroughly confused. If d'Acier wasn't French, she was a cartoonist! And what in the world did the man mean by *take your scalp?* Hadn't her father always told her to ask questions if she wanted to learn something? He had, and she would.

"Mr. d'Acier, why did you refer to Brant as a half-breed?"

"Because that is exactly what he is," Louis replied

blandly. "We never escape the truth by hiding from it, Ms. Marks. Brant's mother was not only one of the most beautiful women I'd ever met, she was also a full-blooded Indian." He smiled in remembrance. "Mohawk to be exact."

"Which is beside the point anyway." Stephen was obviously growing angry. "Where does he get off propositioning my daughter?"

Becoming aware of the curious glances her father's angry voice was drawing to them, Charley slid her hand over his cheek to cover his lips. "Not here, Dad," she urged gently. "There are too many people who would just love to see you explode in public." If only to confirm their own unspoken opinion of us, she added to herself.

Getting control of his temper was a battle for Stephen, but fortunately he won it. Drawing a calming breath, he muttered, "Your son will hear from me about this, Louis. I want an explanation of his behavior, and it had better be a good one."

"I wish you luck." Louis sighed. "I haven't been able to get him to explain himself to me in over ten years." His shoulders moved in a helpless shrug. "My son is his own man, Stephen. He answers to no one."

Studying his handsome face, Charley decided Louis was not in the least disappointed in his son. In fact, she concluded, Louis was inordinately proud of Brant. At that instant Charley knew she wanted to meet the third member of this unusual family, Brant's mother. Casually she let her gaze drift around the room in search of a beautiful, copper-skinned woman. She found none.

"Is your wife here tonight, Mr. d'Acier?" Charley frowned in concentration. "I can't recall meeting her."

"No, Ms. Marks." Louis's smile was gentle but sad. "My wife is dead."

Feeling gauche, Charley did something she rarely ever did; she stammered. "I—I am . . . sorry, sir. I—I didn't know."

"Of course you didn't." Taking possession of her hand, Louis bestowed another kiss on her fingers. "Please don't be upset. I'm not. It has been over three years now and, although the memories still occasionally haunt me, the pain is gone." He gave that odd little shrug again. "At least it is for me. I'm not too sure about Brant. He adored her."

Charley felt a strange twinge in her chest, a twinge too much like pain to be acceptable. Feeling compassion or pain for one of *them* was out of the question and not to be allowed. So Brant had lost a beloved mother, so what? She had, too, and at the vulnerable age of seventeen. Even after eight years Charley still knew moments of crushing grief. But perhaps it had been for the best, for if Charlene Marks had lived, this herd of society animals would have surely trampled her gentle spirit. Louis must have mistaken the glitter of renewed hate in Charley's eyes for compassionate tears, for he squeezed her hand warmly.

"Please, my dear, don't think of it. Brant's continued grief is a good sign really. It reveals a capacity to experience deep affection." His smile again turned sad. "I only pray that the woman Brant finally gives his love to loves him as deeply in return."

Chapter Two

Damn! There she goes with another one!

Brant's narrowed eyes followed Charlott's sensuously moving body as she glided by in the arms of a blond young man, her fourth partner within the last half hour. Absently raising his arm, Brant sipped at the aged Scotch in the glass his fingers seemed determined to crush.

How many have there been? Brant was not thinking about Charlott's dancing partners; he knew exactly how many men had held her in their arms during the hour since he'd walked away from her. Four? Six? Ten? A full dozen? Swine!

Brant was amazed at the fury searing his mind and body. The mere idea of any other man daring to touch her made his blood run hot with rage. She is mine! The thought was shocking. He had met Charlott Marks only a little over an hour ago, and had spent less than fifteen minutes in her company, yet, here he was, feeling as possessive as a jealous husband, and savagely savoring the pleasure to be derived from breaking a few male necks!

The pressure of his fingers on the glass increased, causing a twinge of pain in Brant's hand. A frown drew his brows together, and Brant glanced down. This is ridiculous! he thought, relaxing his death grip on the glass. Lifting it again, he took a long, deep swallow of the potent liquor. His lips pulled into a parody of a smile. This firewater must be going to your head, redskin, he told himself scathingly. Whomever she chooses to share her favors with is none of your concern. She is over twenty-one . . . a good bit over twenty-one. What were you hoping for, a virgin? Brant's smile twisted into a grimace. Logically, no, he answered his own silent question. But ideally, yes. Brant suddenly felt empty, as if he'd lost something very dear and precious to him.

"I've been waiting for a chance to talk to you alone, Brant."

Brant slowly turned at the sound of Stephen Marks's angry voice, glad to be drawn from his disquieting thoughts, even if it was into an argument.

"There's a problem, Stephen?" he asked the older man quietly.

"I hope not," Stephen snorted. "I like you, Brant. Have since the day I met you in your father's office."

"The feeling's mutual, Stephen." Though smooth, Brant's tone held a hint of wariness. "So, let's not beat around any bushes here. Something's bothering you. What is it?"

"I thought you had a thing going with your father's secretary," Stephen said bluntly.

Brant stiffened, every inch of his six-foot-four-inch frame growing taut. He might bestow friendship on a man he respected, but never the right to pry into his personal life. "That is none of your business, Stephen."

"I know that." Stephen nodded his head sharply. "And I couldn't care less . . . about Louis's secretary." Now Stephen infused steel into his voice. "But I do care about Charlott."

"Charlott?" Though it might have seemed impossible, Brant's body grew even more taut. "What are you talking about?" Damn! Brant cursed silently, was he as obvious as all that?

"About you propositioning her!" Stephen gritted through his clenched teeth. "That's what I'm talking about! Are you trying to lose your job with me *and* some of those white teeth?"

There was no way Brant could prevent the grin that revealed those same white teeth. "I'm sure you could probably fire me, Stephen, even though we have a fairly tight contract." Brant's grin disappeared. "But I'm equally sure my teeth are safe." Cool dark eyes swept the older man's burly frame. "You're tough, Stephen." Brant's tone was so silky, an observer might have missed the element of danger in it. Stephen obviously did not. "But not quite tough enough." Brant allowed himself a real smile. "If you start something, I'll have to finish it, and I'd prefer not to do that." One dark eyebrow shot up arrogantly. "Where did you pick up this propositioning story anyway?"

"From Charlott!" Stephen exclaimed. "Damn it,

man, do you think I'd have come to you making threats
on the basis of a rumor I'd overheard?''

That skinny minx! Brant felt torn by a confusing
combination of anger and amusement. Had that flame
top actually gone directly to her father with a report on
his behavior? Apparently she had! Brant felt a sudden
urge to laugh and curse. Controlling both emotions, he
stared down into Stephen's angry eyes. What the hell
could he say to the man?

''Is Charlott in the habit of telling tales out of
school?'' he drawled, hoping for time to compose a
reasonable explanation. Damn it! In truth there *was* no
reasonable explanation! How was he to explain something he didn't understand himself?

''Well, no . . . at least not exactly,'' Stephen blus-
tered. ''I mean, no, of course she's not in the habit of
telling tales!'' He shook his head, as if hoping to settle
his thoughts into some semblance of order. ''And she
didn't actually tell me. She told your father.''

His father! Now Brant did laugh. I'll be damned! As
his laughter subsided Brant sliced a glance at the dance
floor, locating Charley immediately. She was gazing up
at her current partner, an expression of rapt attention on
her breath-stealingly beautiful face. You gorgeous devil,
he addressed her silently. You are really playing with fire
here. Almost as if Charley had received Brant's mental
message, she turned her head to look directly at him, her
eyes gleaming with mischief. Strangely, Brant had the
uncanny sensation that he could hear her teasing voice
responding: I'm not playing with fire . . . I *am* the fire!
You're the one in danger of getting burned.

That would be one pyre I'd gladly fling myself onto!
The thought startled Brant. Was he crazy, or was he

crazy? His mind shied away from the commitment implicit in the thought.

"Are you trying to stare holes through her?" Stephen's irritated tone drew Brant's attention.

"No." Brant's face revealed none of the emotions he was experiencing. "I was searching her face for a clue to her game."

"I don't understand." Stephen frowned. "What game?"

"That's what I'd like to know." Brant smiled sardonically. "But I get this feeling Charlott is weaving her own type of web, for reasons mere mortals like you and I cannot decipher." The shrug that rippled Brant's wide shoulders said more than his actual words. "Time will tell," he murmured fatalistically, then, squaring the shoulders he'd so elegantly shrugged, he stared directly into Stephen's eyes. "All right, I propositioned her. I was not teasing. I was not merely amusing myself with her on the dance floor. I invited her into my bed. I was dead serious." Brant's attitude left Stephen in little doubt that he was indeed serious. "And, at the first opportunity, I will extend the invitation again." A tiny smile softened his words. "I'm sorry, Stephen, but I won't lie to you to make it palatable. The simple fact is, I want your daughter." I'm going to own her, he added to himself.

What *had* he just admitted to? Never in his life had he felt the desire to *own* another person! Not even while in the throes of physical passion had he experienced the slightest urge to own a woman.

There is absolutely no doubt whatever, d'Acier! Your mind has just gone on an extended vacation!

Brant felt Stephen's sigh to the marrow of his bones.

He knew he had created an impossible situation for the older man and for himself. Relenting, he offered Stephen a way out. "If you wish, I'll give you just cause to dissolve our working agreement."

"How would you do that?"

"Default," Brant answered.

"But . . . Brant, you have never defaulted on a contract in your life!"

"No, I haven't," Brant confirmed flatly. "But if you want me off the job, I will." Once again his gaze was steady. "Let's have no misunderstanding here, Mr. Marks." Stephen's eyes widened at the formality. "I fully intend to seduce your daughter."

Stephen's rugged face turned ruddy with what Brant suspected was a combination of anger and embarrassment. Though it didn't show on his own sharply hewn features, Brant was experiencing a similar feeling of embarrassment at the words he had spoken. Damn! Who needed this unprecedented, overwhelming desire to possess one particular woman?

"Well, what's your decision, Stephen?" Brant's disgust with himself was manifested in his low, growling tone. "Do I go on as before? Or do I default?"

Breathing deeply, Stephen hesitated uncertainly a moment, then shook his head in defeat. "Oh, hell, Brant," he sighed. "You know damned well that I don't want anyone but you building my house." Stephen's eyes flashed at the twitch of a smile on Brant's thin lips. "And you don't have to be so damned smug about being the best in the business either!"

"Look, Brant," he went on, "are you so determined to seduce Charley that you'd use force?"

Brant stiffened again. "I never use force, Stephen,"

he gritted out furiously. "Especially with a woman. I give you my word that if Charlott comes to my bed, she will do so willingly."

Brant was not unaware of the incongruity of the conversation; they were discussing Stephen's daughter, for heaven's sake! Apparently Stephen had the same realization, for he smiled sheepishly and shot a glance at the dance floor.

"I feel as though I should punch you in the mouth right here," Stephen finally admitted with a frown. "Yet I also feel admiration for your honesty. Hell, if it were any other woman, I'd be cheering you on, and I know it!" His smile contained a wealth of self-mockery. "The contract between us stands." A grin softened his craggy face. "You do realize that I intend to warn her about your plans?"

"Of course." Brant was not nearly as cool as his tone implied. "I'd be disappointed if you didn't." Now it was Brant's turn to smile in self-mockery. "I do appreciate the awkwardness of the position I've put you in. Your reputation for thinking before you act is well earned."

"Exactly when do you two gentlemen begin patting each other on the back?"

Neither Brant nor Stephen had had an inkling of Charley's approach. Both men froze at the husky sound of her drawling voice.

"Do you make a habit of listening in on other people's conversations?" Brant asked, wondering how long she'd been standing behind them and how much of the conversation she'd heard. If she'd been there long, he mused, the chase could well be over before it ever began.

"I do humbly beg your pardon, Mr. d'Acier, but you

are way off base. As a matter of fact, I was not listening in on your conversation but, had I been, I'm quite sure I would have been bored to distraction.''

"I somehow doubt it.'' Brant offered the dry opinion with a perfectly straight face.

"And why is that?'' Charley inquired with artificial sweetness. Secretly she was savoring the tingle that simply standing close to Brant sent across her naked shoulders. It was almost scary, this deliciously exciting sensation of expectation she felt every time she was near him. Scary, Charley thought, and more than a little confusing, for never had she reacted to a man like this before. After gazing up into his copper-skinned, sharply edged face a moment, Charley lowered her lashes demurely. The effect on Brant was visible for an instant as his eyes flickered in response, then they went blackly remote.

"I wouldn't dream of boring you with the gory details,'' he replied smoothly, ignoring the choking cough Stephen valiantly attempted to hide behind his hand. "Personal business, really,'' he added. "Stephen will tell you all about it later . . . I'm sure.''

Now Charley was really confused, and darned suspicious. They were up to something; she knew it! She glanced from one to the other with avid interest. Brant contrived to appear detached, but her father looked guilty as sin. Charley was suddenly positive they had been discussing her. But why?

"Would you consider dancing with me again?'' Brant's quiet invitation scattered Charley's thoughts. "Even at the risk of your toes?''

"Not to mention my reputation,'' Charley retorted pleasantly.

"Oh, that too," Brant agreed.

"How could any girl refuse an offer like that? Lead on, scout, I'm right behind you."

"Exactly where a properly trained squaw should be," Brant murmured as he drew her into his arms. Then, bending close to her ear, he growled, "Or, right under me." He chuckled at her gasp. "You wanna be my squaw?"

Charley turned her face into his neck to muffle her peal of laughter. This man was absolutely outrageous, but delightfully so. Oh, she was going to love whittling him down to size! She drew the scent of him in as she took several quick, shallow breaths. Tangy aftershave reinforced the musky male essence of him. And every atom in Charley's body responded to that essence. She nuzzled his neck, shivering in reaction to the shudder that rippled through his long body.

"Are you trying to gobble me up?" he teased raggedly.

"Eventually," she promised, moaning softly as his arms tightened convulsively.

"Why do I have this nasty suspicion we're talking about two different things?" Brant leaned back just far enough to look at her warily.

Charley grinned at him. "Possibly because we're talking about two different things?"

One dark eyebrow crept up into an arrogant arch. "You're hoping to add my scalp to your overcrowded belt?"

The "overcrowded" stung! In retaliation Charley tossed back a barb of her own. "No, I'm planning on flying it from my flagpole. Prepare yourself, darling, for the whole world will know you've been well and truly had!'' This time the sweep of her lashes was coolly deliberate. "I'm going to wash you, and starch you, and hang you out to dry."

Brant's twitching lips betrayed the laughter he was swallowing. "And what do you suppose I'll be doing while you're busy washing, starching, and hanging?"

Charley tossed her head, causing her hair to swirl around her shoulders like a dark red cloud. "Loving every minute of it?" She laughed up at him. But her laughter was silenced abruptly as his arms crushed her to his hard chest.

"Oh, I fully intend loving—if not *every* minute! That might be a bit much, even for me." Brant's dark eyes glittered with promise. "But I have no intention of being taken to the laundry." With that declaration he closed his teeth gently on her earlobe. Shifting his head slowly, he brushed his lips across her face to the corner of her mouth, growling in satisfaction when she gasped her shocked pleasure. "*I* was thinking along the lines of having *you* on a platter. A solid gold platter, of course, for breakfast, lunch, dinner, and . . . best of all, a midnight snack."

Charley was quivering with anticipatory shivers. Turning her head swiftly, she nipped at his probing tongue. "That's merely a taste of what you're in for," she whispered warningly.

"If that was the appetizer, I can't wait for the dessert!" Brant punished her by teasing her lips with his, smiling in triumph when she purred softly in appreciation. "You want me to kiss you, don't you?" he taunted huskily, deliberately lifting his head to deny her searching lips access to his mouth.

"Yes." Charley was not surprised at the throaty sound of her voice, but she was a little surprised at the intensity of her physical response to him.

"And I need to kiss you."

Brant's harsh tone sent Charley's heart into high gear. It was almost as if the admission was dragged out of his mouth, against his will, and that pleased her. Why should she be the only one suffering the pangs of confusion and doubt?

"Let's get out of here!"

"To go . . . where?" The question came automatically. At that moment Charley would have gone anywhere with him, so great was her need to know his embrace and the fiery pressure of his mouth.

"Who cares?" Stepping back, Brant pressed his palm lightly to the small of her back to urge her off the floor. "I don't care where we go as long as it's quiet and we can be alone."

With meekness alien to her character, Charley allowed herself to be led toward the exit.

"Charlott! Where are you going?"

The irate sound of her father's voice halted Charley's steps less than three feet from the ballroom entranceway. Where was she going? How could she answer her father's question when she hadn't the vaguest idea of her destination?

"I'm taking Charlott home." Brant answered for her, meeting Stephen's hard-eyed stare coolly.

"To whose home?" the older man demanded.

"The choice is hers," Brant replied quietly.

Charley glanced from Brant's rigidly composed face to her father's, amazement jolting through her at the angry flush on his cheeks. What *was* going on between these two?

"I haven't had a chance to talk to her, and you know it!" Stephen exclaimed angrily.

"Yes, I do." Brant's smile could be described as sardonic. "I'm giving you that chance now." Removing his hand from her back, he stepped away from her. "I'm going for the car, Charlott." Brant glanced at his watch. "If you're not outside in fifteen minutes—" a wry smile twisted his lips—"I'll know you changed your mind."

"But—" Charley began, only to stare, frowning, as Brant strode away through the entranceway. The instant he was out of sight she swung back to her father. "Okay, Dad, let's hear it."

"Brant's admitted to me that he wants you," Stephen said bluntly.

How interesting! Charley's pulse rate accelerated. Oh, she had already known Brant wanted her, he'd made that more than clear, but to have him admit it to her father was very, very interesting. Charley smiled contentedly.

Stephen became alarmed. "I'm not sure I like that calculating look on your face, Charlott. What are you up to?"

"Me?" Charley favored him with her most wide-eyed, innocent look. "Why, nothing!" she protested softly.

"Oh, boy!" Stephen groaned. "Now I know you're up to some trickery. I get the sweats whenever you go into your sweetness and light routine. Honey, Brant d'Acier is *not* a man to play around with," he warned. "He's tough, and experienced with women—all types of women."

Charley attempted to reassure her father. "I will be perfectly all right," she soothed. "I'm not exactly a novice when it comes to men. I can take care of myself."

Stephen's stare was hard for long seconds, then he sighed deeply. "You're an adult, and I can't forbid you to go with him but—" He shook his head in exasperation. "You aren't really going to go with him to his place, are you?"

Charley could no longer contain the laughter that bubbled inside. "Oh, Dad!" she finally gasped. "If I was going to let myself be talked into bed, do you think it would make a difference whose bed it was?"

"Charlott!" Stephen snapped. "I'll be damned if I see anything funny in this! The man is determined to have you. I don't want you hurt."

Charley's laughter died. Smiling gently, she lifted her hand to caress his cheek. "You're pretty special, you know that?" Without waiting for a reply, she went on earnestly. "Dad, trust me. I have no intention of allowing Brant to talk me into bed tonight, neither his nor mine. I'm going to let Brant drive me home, and that's all." Charley scanned the room. "It looks like it won't be long before this circus breaks up." She grinned unrepentantly when he winced at the word *circus*. "If it will set your mind at rest, stop at my apartment on your way home. Okay?"

"You're sure you wouldn't mind?" The question revealed just how very independent Charley was; not even Stephen presumed to intrude into her private life without her invitation.

"I'm positive." Charley smiled impishly. "Cheer up.

I assure you the big, bad Indian is not nearly big enough, or bad enough, to breach the walls of this fortress." Leaning forward, she kissed his cheek. "Now I've got to run. See you later."

With a swirl of her long skirt, Charley spun away from him to walk briskly from the ballroom, fully aware of the assessing male glances that followed her. As her long legs carried her swiftly across the lobby, Charley took little notice of the masculine interest. All her thoughts were on the man waiting for her outside.

"Thank you, and good night." Charley flashed a smile at the doorman as she swept past him, but she really didn't see him. Her gaze was fastened on the gleaming black Cadillac idling at the curb and the tall man leaning indolently against it.

How very like him, she approved. Black hair, black eyes, black attire; what else but a black car? Matches the black designs he has on my virtue! Charley's lips twitched in amusement.

With casual elegance Brant stepped away from the car to swing the door open for her. "Your carriage, Cinderella," he murmured as she crossed the sidewalk.

"Talk about fracturing the fairy tale!" Charley laughed. "Not only is the conveyance the wrong color, I've already been to the ball."

"That's what you think." Brant punctuated the retort by closing the door with a solid-sounding thud.

Relishing the tingle along her spine, Charley sat primly as Brant circled the car then slid onto the plush seat beside her. He certainly was a magnificent-looking son of a gun! Her assessment of his appearance brought a smile to her lips. Tilting his head, Brant studied her a few seconds.

"What's going on under that flame top of yours?" he wondered aloud.

"I was merely thinking what a handsome heathen you are," she informed him honestly. If she had entertained the idea of disconcerting him with her praise, she was to be disappointed, for Brant accepted the compliment with a nod of his head and a devilish grin.

"You ain't exactly chopped liver." Brant's teasing drawl robbed the observation of any sting.

"Please," Charley held up one slim-fingered hand. "Try not to overdo the flattery. It might go to my head!"

Without looking away from her, Brant put the car into drive. "You know perfectly well how beautiful you are." Then he turned away from her to ease the vehicle into the flow of traffic.

"Yes, I do," Charley admitted openly. "All of it thanks to my mother." A wave of her hand dismissed her inherited beauty. "Which is beside the point anyway." Shifting her position, she turned to face him.

"The point?" Giving her a quick glance, Brant frowned. "I don't understand. What point?"

"The meaning of your oblique 'That's what you think.'" Charley lifted one auburn brow. "Or am I better off not knowing?"

Brant's soft laughter did funny things to Charley's spine. "I thought my meaning was obvious." They had stopped for a red light, so he was able to look directly at her. "Your father's banquet was merely the warm-up. The real ball begins shortly."

"No kidding?" Charley fluttered her lashes at him. "Tell me more."

"Uh-uh." Brant shook his head briefly, then returned

his attention to the street as the light changed to green. "I prefer to show you." Even with his face averted, Charley could see his teasing grin. "Your place or mine?"

"Oh, how original!" Her chiding laughter betrayed nothing of the excitement tightening her nerves. "Some sixth sense warns me I'd better let you take me home." *Where I can look forward to my father charging to the rescue,* she added in amused silence.

"Wherever." Brant shrugged in eloquent unconcern. "And where, exactly, is home? I know you don't live in your father's house."

"And how did you discover that bit of information?" she inquired pleasantly.

"He told me."

"But why would Dad tell you that?" Charley demanded curiously, genuinely baffled by her father's unusual lapse of discretion. "I mean, I somehow can't imagine the topic coming up in casual conversation."

"Of course not. He told both my father and me that his primary reason for building the new house was to lure you back home, to live with him."

"So he can keep an eye on me?"

"He didn't say," Brant returned. "But naturally I assumed that was his reason."

Naturally? Hmmm. Narrowing her eyes, Charley stared at Brant's bland expression. *And, naturally, he assumed her father wanted to keep an eye on her because of her reputation.* A flash of anger warred with the growing attraction Charley felt for Brant. *Just who did he think he was to assume anything about her—even if* she had worked very hard at giving him ample reason to do so?

"Are you going to give me some kind of a hint as to where you live?" Brant's question nudged Charley out of her angry thoughts. "Am I at least heading in the right direction?"

Until that moment Charley had been completely unaware of the surroundings outside the luxurious interior of the car. Frowning, she glanced out first the windshield, then her side window. Good grief! Charley muffled a burst of laughter. They were miles from her apartment complex! In an apologetic tone she told him her address, forbidding herself to smile when he groaned in response. It would take another fifteen minutes for him to backtrack, fifteen minutes closer to the time when her father would arrive at the apartment!

Content with the knowledge that she would not have to face a prolonged wrestling match, Charley relaxed against the supple leather upholstery of the car seat. "So, you build houses," she said brightly.

"Among other things." Brant's suspicious tone delighted Charley. Perfect, she nearly purred aloud. I'll pick the time, and I'll pick the place, Running Bear, she promised him silently.

"Other things?" she prompted.

"Other buildings," he clarified. "From small summer retreat A-frames, to multiple office and apartment complexes."

"Really?" Charley was impressed, and made no attempt at concealing it. Ability and achievement were the only things that *did* impress her.

"Yes, really," Brant said flatly. "Now tell me how interested you are in how I earn my living."

The hint of contempt in his tone brought Charley's head around to face him. "But I am interested!" she protested. "And, if this car is any indication, I'd guess you earn a very good living."

"You'd guess correctly," he confirmed. "Although I'm not a millionaire . . . yet." Once again he drew the car to a stop at a red light. With a sardonic twist to his lips, he turned to gaze directly at her. "You like money. Don't you, Charlott?"

"Doesn't everybody?" Somehow she managed to keep her annoyance from her voice. Once again, he was making incorrect assumptions about her, and she longed to set him straight. But not yet.

"Certainly." Brant agreed readily, too readily. "But not everybody has the wherewithal to spend it at the rate you appear capable of."

"Then isn't it nice that I do have the wherewithal?" she asked carelessly.

Once again the light changed to green, only this time Brant's shifting of gears was not quite so smooth. Everything about him, from the way he held his head, to the rigid line of his shoulders, spoke of his disapproval, and they finished the drive in silence.

As they neared the apartment complex Charley directed Brant to the large tenant parking area. By the time Brant brought the car to a full stop, she had decided she would not invite him in. Brant quickly disabused her of that notion.

"Are you too angry to offer me a nightcap or coffee?" he asked as she reached for the door release.

Was she? Charley asked herself as she slowly turned

back to look at him. The mere sight of him set her pulse racing. Allowing a small smile, she shook her head. Still, she couldn't resist a tiny dig of her own.

"Are you too contemptuous of me to accept the offer if I extended it?"

Brant was out of the car in an instant.

Chapter Three

What a perfectly gorgeous night! The thought struck Charley as she stepped from the car onto the macadam parking lot. The warm evening air gently caressed her exposed shoulders and arms, and the heady scent of roses from the bushes that outlined the complex grounds tantalized her senses.

As they strolled to the entrance, Brant's light touch at her waist sent a shiver along her spine. The balmy air and the sweet scent of the roses could not begin to stir her senses the way the tall man beside her did! The thought brought a smile to Charley's lips, which she hid by making a production of searching in her beaded bag for her door key.

"Very nice," Brant remarked as they crossed the starkly elegant lobby to the double elevators.

"Yes, isn't it," Charley tossed over her shoulder,

stepping into the elevator when the doors hissed open. Had there been a whisper of condemnation in his tone? she mused, touching the button for the seventh floor. Well, of course there had, she chided herself. Like everyone else, Brant believed she was spending her father's money with a vengeance! Wasn't that what she wanted everyone to believe? Yes . . . but . . . Charley caught herself up short. Hold it, girl! There are no buts. Brant d'Acier is no different from any of the others! Like a shiny red apple, he looks delicious, but underneath he is as rotten as the rest in the society barrel. She thought of her former fiancé and the way he had betrayed her trust, and hardened her heart against Brant.

"Expensive too." Charley offered the information with coolly deliberate flippancy. The elevator came to a smooth halt, the doors hissed open, and she sailed by him with her head held high. "I like expensive things." To catch his reaction, Charley slanted him a sideways glance as she came to a stop at the door to her apartment. Brant's lips were compressed tightly in disapproval, his eyes were narrowed, and a tiny frown line bridged the gap between his eyebrows. Even though it was exactly the reaction she had aimed for, Charley had to fight down a sudden urge to smooth the frown away with her fingers. Her own ambivalence shook her from the inside out, and she had to concentrate on keeping her fingers steady while inserting her key into the lock.

Damn! What was the matter with her? Charley examined her mixed emotions as she turned the key and pushed the door open. She had been escorted home like this numerous times, by a wide variety of men, yet never had any one of them affected her like Brant. After turning on the indirect overhead lighting, she swept into the minuscule foyer and down the two shallow steps to the large square living room.

"What would you like?" Charley asked over her shoulder, dropping her beaded bag onto a highly polished oak coffee table.

"Directions to the bedroom."

"Wh—at?!" Spinning around, Charley stared at Brant. He was laughing at her! A scathing retort formed in her mind, then she swallowed it. Okay, Sitting Bull, you caught me on that one, Charley admitted. But, in the end, you'll know you've met your personal Little Big Horn. Tilting her head, Charley smiled mysteriously. "You're sleepy?" she asked guilelessly.

"I don't think sleepy quite describes my present condition," Brant drawled huskily.

"No, of course not!" Long lashes fluttered innocently over laughing blue eyes. "You're thirsty. Wasn't that the request? A nightcap or coffee?" Kicking off her sandals, she padded across the thick champagne-gold carpet to the kitchen, aware that Brant was right behind her. "Name your poison," she invited. In an effort to conceal her nervousness, she swung open a cabinet door and, with a sweeping wave of her hand, indicated the impressive array of bottles inside.

With obvious reluctance Brant shifted his gaze from Charley's face, a wry smile curving his lips. "I think I'd better settle for coffee. My libido's humming along fine; it doesn't need an added kick."

Flustered by his frankness, disturbed by his very closeness, Charley raked her mind for a suitable retort and came up blank. She could barely think straight; witty rejoinders were far beyond her capabilities at the moment. Staring into Brant's unreadable dark eyes, Charley felt her body sway toward the lure of his and caught herself up short. Stop it at once! The idea was for *you* to play with *him,* not the other way around!

"Coffee! Yes, of course. It will only take a minute!" Slamming the cabinet door closed, Charley grabbed for the glass pot of the automatic coffeemaker. "How do you like it? Strong? Dark? Medium?" She was babbling, and she knew it. Cool down, girl, she chided herself scathingly. He's only a man, for heaven's sake! Somehow managing to steady her hand, Charley filled the pot with cold water and poured it into the machine.

"Yes."

Charley frowned. What did he mean, yes? And did she detect a hint of laughter in his voice? If Brant d'Acier was laughing at her . . . she'd clobber him! Charley slanted an angry glance at him. "Yes, what?"

"Yes, I like it strong and dark." Though Brant's face and tone were devoid of inflection, his black eyes glittered with amusement.

"You find something funny?" she asked, forcing herself to remain calm.

Brant nodded his head at the coffeemaker. "To get it strong and dark, shouldn't you put some coffee grounds in there somewhere?" he wondered with contrived seriousness.

Charley blinked once, then turned back to glare at the inoffensive machine. How could she be so stupid? She was never inept, and never, ever flustered by a man! Feeling more than a little ridiculous, Charley stood watching as hot, clear water trickled into the glass container.

"I'll—I'll start over as soon as the water runs through," she muttered tersely.

With a tiny click Brant flicked the switch to Off. "Forget it. I'm really not thirsty." He clasped her upper arm and turned her around to face him fully. Somber black eyes examined her features minutely before settling on her slightly parted lips. "At least I'm not thirsty for booze or coffee." His eyes holding hers captive, Brant lowered his head. "I was thinking along the lines of liquid honey," he murmured an instant before his lips brushed hers.

At the feather touch of his mouth Charley stiffened with resistance. This was not going at all as she'd planned. *She* was supposed to be the one calling the shots here! The long, roundabout drive to her apartment had given ample time for her blood to cool, leaving her clearheaded and amazed at her own reaction to Brant on the dance floor. Had she actually been willing to go *any*where with him? She had, and that in itself frightened her. She simply could not afford this self-indulgence. Yet it required every ounce of willpower she possessed to turn her head to avoid his mouth.

"Brant, no! I—I'm . . ."

"Why not?" Brant's voice, rough with impatience, interrupted her unformed protest. "Why should I be the only drone denied the honey?"

His question shocked her to her senses. Once again he was making assumptions about her loose moral character. That Charley had not only allowed him to make such assumptions but had encouraged it as well was dismissed as irrelevant in the heat of that moment. Like all the rest of his ilk, Brant couldn't be bothered to scratch the surface to examine what might or might not be hiding underneath. Disappointment sharpened her tongue.

"Why?" she asked. "Because you simply don't turn this particular queen bee on."

"That's a lie, and you know it." The accusation brought a flood of pink into Charley's cheeks. The pink deepened as he went on lazily. "I could have had you on the dance floor, had I been so inclined, and you know that too. Exactly what kind of game are you playing here, Charlott?" Before she could even protest, Brant added smoothly, "I make a much better partner when I know the ground rules." His gaze slid over her slowly. "Must I first offer gifts?" Again Charley was not to be allowed an indignant protest. "What is it you want?" he asked softly. "Name it. And, if it's at all possible, I'll produce it."

Stunned speechless, Charley merely stared at Brant. Produce it? *Produce it!* This . . . this creature was actually offering to *buy* her! Never mind that she had knowingly fostered the idea that she was up for grabs; why wasn't he more perceptive? Charley thought irrationally. Suddenly she wanted to cry like a lost child—and that was not at all like her!

What was happening to her? The question stabbed at Charley's mind as she stared at Brant d'Acier's confident expression. And where was her father anyway? She had assumed that he'd be here by now, charging to her rescue. And she needed her father now, desperately. Brant's very proximity was a threat to her.

Brant moved languidly to stand within inches of her. Lifting one dark brow, he smiled knowingly.

"What is it you want?" he repeated softly, his smile saying more than his actual words.

He knows. The realization seared through Charley. Brant knows that I'm yearning to be crushed to him. He knows, because he can see my lips quivering with the need to explore his. Does he also know that I ache with an unfamiliar emptiness? An emptiness that I'm suddenly positive only he can fill? This last thought frightened Charley into action and speech.

"Nothing!" she blurted out, swinging away from him. "You have nothing I want!" She walked away from him toward the living room, but he followed right behind her.

"Oh, Charlott," he scolded gently. "Your nose is gonna grow, and everyone will know." Closing in, he again came to a stop within inches of her. "And here I was, giving you credit for having the courage of honesty."

Where are you, Dad? The cry for help remained silent as Charley gazed up into Brant's dark eyes, now alight with devilish laughter. Feeling cornered, Charley threw caution to the wind.

"Okay, you win, I'll tell you what I want. Everything! I want everything. And the best of it." With a wide sweep of her arm Charley indicated her immediate surroundings, then let her hand flutter down the length of her torso. "I am not blind, Mr. d'Acier. I know that what you see when you look at me is a rather appealing package." Lifting her head arrogantly, Charley stared directly into Brant's eyes. "I am beautiful."

"Modest too." Despite the joke, Brant frowned. "And you plan to use your beauty to acquire this 'everything'?"

Why couldn't he be different? Ruthlessly ignoring the hurt he'd caused her, she went on. "Of course. Why not?"

"Charlott!" From his expression, Charley had the distinct impression that Brant was fighting the urge to slap her. Instead, his arm snaked out to coil around her waist, hauling her roughly to him. She was allowed no time for defensive action or protest as, tangling his fingers in the hair at the back of her neck, he anchored her head securely and punished her mouth with his lips. Within seconds those hard lips mastered her own and her mouth opened, welcoming the ravishment of his searching tongue.

Rationality, common sense, self-preservation, all fled from consideration; Charley drank as greedily from Brant as he did from her. Even the realization that she was slowly being lowered to the plush carpeting failed to worry her.

Bemused, drowning in a sea of hot sensuality, she felt the soft fibers being crushed beneath her back even as his chest crushed the softness of her breasts.

"Lord! You are just as exciting as I knew you would be!" Brant groaned, sliding his lips from hers to explore her satiny skin with his mouth and tongue and teeth.

Her body rejoicing in the heaviness of his, Charley moved her head restlessly on the luxurious wool rug, creating a static that was nothing compared to the electrical shock generated by the line of stinging kisses Brant drew down her neck to the wildly beating pulse in her throat. A violent shudder went through her body at the touch of his tongue and a moan of pleasure sighed through her lips when that moist tip skipped to the V neck of her gown.

Lifting her arms with sudden urgency, Charley raked her fingers through the crisp strands of Brant's hair, her nails lightly digging into his scalp in an unspoken plea.

Brant's understanding was immediate. Drawing one palm up from where it rested against her thigh, he carefully brushed the flimsy chiffon aside to expose one perfectly shaped breast.

"You *are* beautiful," he murmured deeply, tormenting her and himself by skimming his lips over the aching crest before taking full possession of it.

"Brant!" Charley's gasping cry was wrenched from the depths of her being, from the fiery core of her femininity. Completely out of control, she arched her back in an effort to give him full access to her.

The sound of the doorbell was a strident intrusion. So lost was Charley in the newly discovered world of sensuality that the bell rang several times before she realized it must be her father at the door.

"Damn." Brant cursed with soft savagery as he pushed himself up and away from her. "Don't answer it," he ordered softly.

"I—I must." Feeling bereft, Charley bit her lip as she stared into Brant's passion-flushed face. "I—I think it's my father." I also think I must be losing my mind. Get off the floor, you fool! she chastized herself. Almost as if to nudge her into action, the bell pealed once more.

"Oh, hell!" Frustration scored Brant's face, yet his fingers were gentle as he slipped the chiffon back into place over her breast. "I might suggest that your father's timing is lousy," he murmured, springing to his feet. "But, from your expression, I somehow think you'd disagree." With a shrug Brant reached down to help her to her feet.

Embarrassed, Charley averted her eyes, making a production of straightening her gown as she hurried to the door.

"What took you so long?" Stephen growled, charging into the room. "Or do I know the answer to that already?" he added, catching sight of Brant. "You don't waste any time. Do you?" he snarled at Brant.

In contrast to the older man, Brant appeared coolly collected. "I did warn you, Stephen," Brant observed mildly. "As you will note from your daughter's lack of hysteria, there has been no pressure applied here."

Stunned speechless, Charley stared into Brant's mocking black eyes. No pressure applied? she thought wildly. No, maybe not in the form of physical violence, but this man could apply emotional pressure by performing the simple act of breathing in and out!

"I'm . . ." Charley had to pause to wet her lips. "I'm fine, Dad. Really," she insisted at Stephen's skeptical look. "And Brant was just leaving," she added, giving Brant a superior smile. "Weren't you, Brant?"

"I suppose I was," he drawled with infuriating aplomb. "And you were going to show me to the door, weren't you?" Brant challenged.

Charley couldn't help herself; she laughed in concession. "I suppose I was," she mimicked sweetly. "I'll be with you in a minute, Dad," she assured her obviously confused father as she preceded Brant to the door.

Before following Charley, Brant walked over to Stephen, his right hand extended. "Is our appointment still on for Tuesday, Stephen?"

"The appointment stands, Brant."

"Very well." Brant clasped Stephen's hand briefly. "I'll see you Tuesday. Good night, Stephen." Without waiting for a response, he turned and strode to the door.

Charley heard her father's murmured "good night,"

then met his glance. "If you don't mind, honey, I'll help myself to a brandy," he said. Charley smiled; how like her father to give her a few moments' privacy for Brant's leavetaking.

"Your father has both guts and class," Brant complimented quietly.

And that surprises you? Charley bit back the retort. Damn, why did she continue to hope this man would prove himself different from the rest of the men she knew?

"In spades," she assured him icily. "He comes from peasant stock . . . good, decent people."

Brant's dark brows arched. "Are you taking potshots at my forebears?"

"You can read anything you wish into my remark." Charley shrugged.

Brant's soft chuckle came as a complete surprise. "You are a snob!"

"Me . . . ! I!" Charley exclaimed. "I certainly am not!"

"Then you have reason to believe the Mohawks are not good, decent people?" he asked dryly.

Mohawks? Charley stared at him blankly an instant then, appalled, shook her head vigorously. "No, of course not!"

"Aaah," Brant sighed. "I see. Your little dart was aimed at my Philadelphia ancestors." This time his sigh was exaggerated. "Whether you are aware of it or not, Ms. Marks, you are definitely a snob. The question is, why?"

"Do you make a habit of poking your aristocratic nose into the personalities of all your new acquaintances, Mr. d'Acier?" she inquired coldly.

"No." Brant's shoulders moved in a shrug; the smile that curved his lips warned of the taunt about to be delivered. "Only those I have sexual designs on; I like to explore the mind as well as the body." Brant's smile grew into a grin when Charley gasped softly. "You see how intrepid I am?" he teased.

Charley was unamused. "I have no desire to be explored—either psychologically or physically." Twisting the ornate doorknob, she swung the door open. "Good night . . . Mr. d'Acier."

With a casual flick of his hand Brant nudged the door shut again. "Not quite yet," he murmured with grim intent. "I have at least ten thousand questions, but"—he chuckled at her alarmed expression—"for the moment I'll be satisfied if you answer just one of them."

"And that one is?" Charley asked warily.

"You said you want everything?" he goaded. At her brief nod he rapped out, "What everything?"

Charley fancied she could hear the spring snap on the trap she'd so flippantly set for herself. Once again she called herself a fool for starting this silliness. How could she answer him when she'd told him she wanted "everything" out of pure perversity? Still, Charley refused to reveal her true feelings to a man who was so ready to think the worst of her. "The usual everything," she answered vaguely.

"Not good enough," Brant retorted. "You want something; I want something. I know you can give me what *I* want. I'm not leaving until I clearly understand what *you* want. So . . . what everything?"

Utterly frustrated, she waved one hand ineffectually. "Oh, *everything!*" she snapped. "The earth, and all the best things on it!" Amazed at her own lack of control,

Charley drew a deep, calming breath. "That is absolutely all I have to say on the subject. My father is waiting. Good *night*, Mr. d'Acier."

With a cool that was maddening, Brant slid his arms around Charley's waist and drew her against him. "If you call me Mr. d'Acier again, I might revert to type and go on the warpath." The tip of his nose touching hers, Brant asked teasingly, "How would you like to be ravished?"

"Have you forgotten the one-man cavalry in my kitchen?" Gazing up at him, Charley stared at the tiny image of herself reflected in the dark mirror of his eyes. "All I have to do is squeak and he'll come charging to my rescue." Becoming lost in those black depths, she felt a curl of excitement as the image drew nearer. The curl tightened into a knot of nervous anticipation when Brant's mouth touched hers.

"I haven't forgotten anything," he murmured. "Including your response to me a little while ago." The tip of his tongue came out to tease her lower lip; a low growl rumbled in his throat at her involuntary moan. "Squeak away, if you can."

Of course she could not; the pressure of his mouth against hers prevented any sound except the softest whimper of pleasure. This man certainly knew his way around a lady's lips! Ignoring the warning bells clanging inside her head, Charley slid her arms around his strong neck and returned his kiss for all she was worth. Apparently she was worth quite a bit, for his arms tightened compulsively and her whimper was returned in the form of a low groan.

The intrusion of Brant's tongue into the moist warmth

of her mouth was no intrusion at all, but a searing pleasure. Thoroughly mastered, Charley clung to Brant's neck and mouth. Aching for more, and still more, she arched her body into the tall frame that curved over her, growing weak with need for closer contact with the rock hardness of him. Only the necessity of breathing finally separated them. Gasping, Charley came back to reality when Brant lifted his head to stare at her through eyes smoky with passion.

"I'm not leaving." Brant's rough, uneven whisper told of her effect on him. "Send Daddy on his way so we can be alone." His peremptory tone brought her to her senses quicker than anything else could have.

Breaking free of Brant's arms, Charley pulled the door open, this time holding on firmly to the knob, albeit with trembling fingers. Through lips still quivering from the feel and taste of his, she somehow managed a firm dismissal. "It's late, and I'm sure my father must be getting bored with looking at my kitchen walls by now." As she stepped farther back Brant moved closer.

"Charlott . . ."

"Brant, please," Charley quickly interrupted, not wanting to hear, and perhaps be swayed by, whatever he had to say. "It *is* getting late. Please, just go."

Brant's eyes bored into hers for long seconds before he shrugged and stepped back. "I don't like losing, not even the first round." His low voice held a trace of lingering passion. "When can I look forward to round two?"

Shaking her head, Charley began, "I don't think . . ."

"Don't say it. Like it or not, there's a strong physical

attraction between us that I have no intention of ignoring.'' His gaze dropped to her lips. ''I want you. You want me.'' A self-assured smile tugged at his mouth as he raised his eyes to hers. ''Sooner or later it's going to happen. I'd prefer that it be sooner. So, when can I see you?''

The small distance separating them had restored a portion of her equilibrium, and Charley studied Brant's confident features with rising indignation. How dare he decide *it* was going to happen? If *it* ever happened *she'd* decide when—and with whom! Yet, if she was ever going to get rid of him, she supposed she'd have to acquiesce, or at least appear to.

''Tomorrow?'' Brant prodded.

''I—I don't know.'' She infused a wistful, confused note into her voice. ''I seem to have gone completely blank. I can't remember if I have a previous engagement or not.'' Charley was lying through her teeth; she was fully aware that she'd made no dates for the following evening. ''Why don't you call me after I've had a chance to check my calendar?''

Brant's eyes narrowed with disbelief, but after consideration, he nodded sharply. ''Okay, I'll call you.'' His smile was exciting and frightening at the same time. ''You had better answer.'' Moving abruptly, he strode out of the apartment. ''Sweet dreams, Ms. Marks,'' he called softly over his shoulder.

Fighting a sudden, inexplicable urge to call him back, Charley watched the supple movement of Brant's long body as he traversed the hall. He didn't look back until he reached the end of the corridor. Then, with a jaunty wave of his hand, he blew her a kiss and stepped out of sight into the elevator. Sighing softly for no explainable reason, she closed the door and walked slowly to the kitchen to join her father.

The earth, and all the best things on it. The phrase echoed inside Brant's head as he drove along the deserted streets to his town house near the Delaware River.

Brant touched the button that activated the electrically controlled overhead door on the garage adjacent to the tall, narrow house. Entering the house through the kitchen, Brant walked unerringly through the dark room to the equally dark hallway and up the steps to his bedroom at the front of the building. Flicking on the light switch with one hand and pulling off his black bow tie with the other, Brant grimaced at his own reflection in the wide mirror above the ebony double dresser. A huge bed opposite the dresser took up most of the room's floor space.

"You must be losing your touch, d'Acier," he informed the scowling image in the looking glass. "When you can't make first base with a woman who's racked up a higher score than a fourteen-inning ballgame, there has got to be something wrong with your approach."

His lips twisting into a sardonic smile, Brant turned to the closet built into the wall and neatly hung his jacket on a wooden hanger. But he knew Charlott had responded to him. The memory of just how passionate that response had been halted the motion of his fingers as they lowered the zipper on his trousers.

"Damn!"

He completed the motion and slid the fine material

over his long, muscular flanks. Carefully aligning the sharp creases, he draped the pants over the wooden bar of another hanger and hung them beside the jacket.

Why had she denied him? Brant's shiny black dress shoes hit the closet floor with a thud, his silk socks arched into the opened hamper beside the dresser and were followed seconds later by the ruffled shirt and navy blue briefs. Why had she denied him? The question continued to jab at Brant's mind as he brushed his teeth. The fact that Stephen had appeared at her door at a most untimely moment had nothing to do with her denial and Brant knew it. With or without Stephen's arrival, he would have been refused.

But why? Standing under the stinging hot spray of the shower, Brant raked his mind for an answer. From what he'd read about her in the papers, and inadvertently overheard, he was sure Charlott Marks was the easiest, if the most expensive, woman in town.

He shut the water off with an abrupt twist of his wrist. Cursing softly, he rubbed himself dry then stomped into the bedroom. He sighed as he slid between the brown and white striped sheets. Lying perfectly still, Brant silently ordered his bunched muscles into relaxation.

After deciding he would not think about her, Brant found himself unable to think about anything else. The notion of another man, let alone a legion of other men, putting their hands on her, possessing her, filled his throat with the taste of acid.

"Oh, hell!"

Flinging an arm over his eyes, Brant willed the image of Charley from his consciousness. The image laughed, fluttering dark lashes over shimmering blue eyes.

God, he wanted her! He had wanted her from the

minute he'd drawn her into his arms on the dance floor. Now, having had a taste of the sweetness of her, Brant wanted her to the point of actual pain. His body writhed with renewed desire. He muttered a harsh expletive and kicked the sheet to the foot of the bed. He would have her, even if it cost him his friendship with her father.

The silent vow sent Brant's thoughts veering in another direction. What was wrong with Stephen Marks anyway? He had to be aware of Charlott's lifestyle. Yet he had taken exception to Brant's propositioning her. Had Stephen been putting on an act for appearance's sake? Brant shook his head. Stephen was too honest to play that kind of game. Then why had he become unglued at Brant's determination to become Charlott's lover? As to that, why had Charlott suddenly become so particular in her choice of lovers? Damn it! *Why* had she denied *him?*

The questions tormented Brant as the blackness of night slowly mellowed to the first faint pink of morning.

During those lonely hours Charley was likewise engaged in self-torment.

Her father had left soon after Brant, having first delivered a stern lecture on the virtue of virtue.

"Damned if I can figure out what you're playing at, Charley, but whatever it is, I know I don't like it!" he'd scolded tiredly. "Why anyone would make a career out of creating a bad reputation is beyond my limited intellectual range! You're deliberately hurting yourself, and I don't like it!"

"I know what I'm doing, Dad," Charley assured him calmly. "And whether you approve or not, so do you."

"I thought I did," Stephen grunted. "I never liked it,

but I thought I understood it. Now I'm not so sure.'' His gaze caressed Charley's face. ''Honey, I'm afraid that if you fool around with Brant d'Acier, you are going to get hurt.''

Going to get hurt? Stifling a groan against her lace-edged pillow, Charley mentally repeated her father's warning. *Going* to get hurt? One brief skirmish with Brant d'Acier and she was already hurting! Brant had so effortlessly reawakened needs and desires she had long ago divorced herself from. She wanted him! Really wanted him!

The realization was both thrilling and terrifying.

Chapter Four

Sitting slouched on the high stool, Charley stared listlessly out through the floor-to-ceiling windows of her studio. The sunlight was pure gold; the sky was bright blue; Charley felt dull brown.

After a restless two and a half hours' sleep, she had been awakened by a phone call at seven-fifteen. Though she was awake by the second ring, Charley had ignored the shrill summons; if it was something important, she reasoned, whoever it was would call back later; if it was not important, it didn't matter anyway.

After curling onto her side Charley had spent fifteen minutes trying to recapture oblivion. But she gave up in disgust when her gritty eyelids refused to stay closed. Dragging her body off the bed and under the shower, she had attempted to motivate herself by counting down the number of days left until the exhibition.

That had been over four hours ago. Now, having accomplished absolutely nothing at all, Charley stared at the canvas propped at eye level on an easel in front of her. Creative inspiration had proved elusive.

"Oh, shut up!" she exclaimed when the phone rang.

Even as she snarled the order her answering machine clicked on, the tape replaying her recorded message for what had to be the sixth time within the last hour. Lips tightening in determination, Charley listened to Brant's impatient voice.

"Damn it, Charlott! Where the hell are you?"

That was it, no elaboration, no message, simply that one frustrated question. The messages had all been recorded at one time or another during Brant's first eight or nine calls.

"I've gone to Alaska!" Charley shouted. "I hear it's *quiet* there!" The phone rang again. "That does it!" Jumping off the stool, she stormed across the room to the instrument, snatching up the receiver even as the message began playing its tired litany. "I'm not home!" she snapped into the mouthpiece.

"You'd better be home." The throaty feminine voice held both a warning and amusement. "And you'd better be working too."

"Oh, hi, Dani!" Charley greeted her agent unenthusiastically. "Sorry for snapping, but this darned phone has been driving me bananas all morning."

"Apology accepted," Dani drawled. "Now answer my question. Are you working?"

"No," Charley responded frankly. "My intentions were sterling when I sat down before my easel, but they've tarnished during the hours since then."

"Am I speaking to *the* Charlott Marks?" There was

puzzlement in Dani's voice. "The same Charlott Marks whose concentration would not be affected by a Sherman tank rolling through her studio?"

Charley sighed. Dani was right. Normally Charley had no trouble concentrating on her work, to the exclusion of everything else. She knew only too well why the previous hours had proved the exception to the rule. The reason could be summed up in two words: Brant d'Acier.

"Charley?" Dani's voice interrupted Charley's wandering thoughts.

"I'm here, Dani." Charley forced a light laugh. "At least I think I am. What was the question?" she hedged.

"Why aren't you working? The sands are running out of the glass, you know."

"Have I ever let you down?" Charley answered.

"Noooo," Dani crooned. "But then, there's a first time for everything." Before Charley could respond, Dani added, "I only pray *this* will not be your first time!"

"It won't be." There was a note of assurance in Charley's voice. "There are only two more to go . . . besides the one I'm doing now, of course."

"Only two more, she says!" Dani groaned.

"Dani, I will finish in time," Charley promised. "Trust me."

"I do." Dani's acceptance was an accolade to Charley's competence, and Charley knew it.

"Thanks, slave driver." Charley laughed easily. "Now, suppose you hang up and let me go back to staring at the canvas."

"Your wish . . . and all that," Dani quipped. "But will you bite off my head if I check in with you later?"

"Not if you promise to make it much later." All the

laughter disappeared from Charley's tone. "I'm going to finish this today if it takes me till midnight," she vowed grimly.

"Glad to hear it!" Dani applauded. "Buzz you then."

The instant Charley heard the dial tone after Dani hung up, she disconnected the phone wire from the jack. That line of communication satisfactorily severed, she averted her eyes from the canvas and escaped into the kitchen in search of sustenance. Perhaps, she thought, her breakfast of three cups of coffee and the tip of one fingernail had not been conducive to creative endeavor.

Thirty minutes later, fortified by a cream cheese and olive sandwich and a bracing cup of herbal tea, Charley was again perched on the stool, staring out the window. Damn! Why was she so dissatisfied with the painting? Charley swung her gaze to the large canvas. For all intents and purposes it was complete, yet there was something missing—but what? Critically, objectively, Charley examined her work.

She had deliberately muted the background with dark, somber shades to draw the eye to the figure of a woman in the forefront of the scene. Though the woman's garments were obviously cheap and well-worn, they could have been the raiment of a queen, so regally did she wear them. Her face was still young, but devoid of all innocence and naiveté, those softer qualities replaced by experience and determination. Standing straight, her shoulders back, the woman was positioned before a high window, looking out over the tall spires of a large city, her expression telling the viewer of her intention to conquer all she surveyed.

Complete. The story was all there in the scene she had created. Yet . . . Charley shook her head. Something was nagging at the edge of her consciousness, some little, left-out thing that wanted to be included. Slowly Charley inched her gaze over the canvas. What was it? What had she left unsaid by her brush?

Everything. *The earth, and all the best things on it.*

Charley could actually hear the exasperation in her voice as she flung the words at Brant. Why think of that now? She frowned, then a broad smile lit her face. That's it!

Lethargy vanished as, with a burst of energy, Charley set to work to add the final touch to the canvas. It was so very simple, yet so right! Her full concentration restored, Charley worked, heedless of the passage of time, until, signing her name with a flourish, she stepped back to study the finished product.

The background was still darkly somber, the woman still gazed with challenge at the city, but now her slim hand rested on a large globe, as if promising herself not only the city, but all that the earth had to offer.

Buoyant with her accomplishment, Charley stripped off her paint-smeared jeans and pullover and treated herself to a long bath. Calmed and relaxed, she stepped into lace panties and slipped a finely pleated, gauzy cotton caftan over her head. Sliding her feet into sandals that consisted of two thin leather straps and a sole, she ambled out of her bedroom to the kitchen unmindful of the damp, tangled mass of auburn waves bouncing on her shoulders.

While preparing, and subsequently eating, a meal of broiled veal chops and tossed salad, Charley visualized in minute detail the two paintings she still had to do to complete the agreed-upon number. One would be ethereal in nature: a very work-a-day suspension bridge spanning the distance between the earth and the other side of the rainbow. The other would be a celebration of physical perfection: a beautifully proportioned ballet dancer leaping into the air.

Thinking of the work at hand brought to mind the gallery where the work would be displayed, and from there Charley's thoughts wandered to the owner of that very prestigious gallery: Dani! Dani had promised-threatened?—to call again later! And Charley had not plugged the wire back into the jack in her studio!

Once the wire was firmly in place again, Charley blithely ignored her messages and closed the door on the workroom. Surely she'd earned a drink to sip while she watched her favorite news team on TV. A glass of chenin blanc in hand, she tuned in to the newscaster, who was already five minutes into the eleven o'clock report.

Charley was staring pensively at the small screen when the trill of the door chime intruded. Wary because of the lateness of the hour, Charley approached the door cautiously. She could guess who it was, of course, still, she took the time to peer out the tiny peephole. As she'd expected, Brant d'Acier filled her field of vision. With a sigh of acceptance Charley disengaged the chain, slid back the bolt, and twisted the knob on the dead lock.

"Has business been slow?" Brant attacked her the minute she opened the door, confusing and angering her at the same time.

"Business?" Charley frowned, backing up automatically as he entered uninvited. "Slow?" she repeated. "Brant, what are you talking about?"

Brant took the two shallow steps in one and strode to the middle of the living room before whipping around to glare at her. His eyes were glittering with rage. "Are you low on funds?" he rasped.

"Are you out to lunch?" Charley retorted. "What *is* your problem, Mr. d'Acier?"

"My problem, Ms. Marks?" Brant echoed very softly. He stalked back to where she stood at the base of the steps. "My 'problem' seems to be with a disconnected phone, not to mention a disconnected bimbo!" Ignoring her yelp of outrage, Brant continued. "Where were you all day and night? And why has your phone service been cut off?" Placing his balled fists on his hips, Brant leaned close to her face. "Do you need money?" he demanded.

"No, I don't need money!" Charley spat back at him. "And most especially I don't need yours!" Then, lowering her voice, she advised, "Back it up, d'Acier."

"D'Acier?" Brant's lids narrowed warningly. "D'Acier?" he repeated softly. "*Mr*. d'Acier to the likes of you, sweetheart!" His term of endearment was definitely not endearing! He didn't back up either! Lowering his face to within an inch of hers, Brant grated, "You're the one who asked me to call you, remember? Of course, I should have realized I'd have to take my place at the end of the line. Do you have a numbered ticket machine outside your bedroom door? Do you give green stamps?"

Charley felt the shock from his verbal blow all the way down to her feet. This . . . this heathen was calling her a . . . "*What?*" Charley demanded, pushing against his chest with all the strength her slender arms possessed. Not surprisingly, Brant remained rock steady. His hands shot up to capture her wrists, anchoring her hands to his body.

Refusing to give him the satisfaction of watching her struggle, Charley went still, hating, loving, the fiery tingle scorching her palms from the contact with his warm body. "You . . . you bas—"

"Watch it!" Brant growled. "I don't take kindly to being called names."

"But I'm supposed to meekly accept being called a . . . a bimbo and a hooker?" Charley sputtered. "Just who do you think you are? Barging in here like a wildman, making all kinds of accusations? And, for your information, my phone has not been disconnected by the phone company! *I* disconnected it. The damned thing was interfering with my concentration, and getting on my nerves!"

"What, or whom, were you so busy concentrating on?" Impossible as it seemed, Brant's anger doubled. "Who was with you all day?" he demanded harshly. "Or, should I ask, who all?"

"You . . . I . . . damn it! I haven't seen a single blessed soul all day!" Charley shouted. "I was busy—" Hold it! Charley bit off her explanation just in time; had she actually been on the point of blowing her cover? God! Never had a man, or anyone else, rattled her so! Brant's fingers tightened around her wrists when Charley clamped her lips together.

"Busy doing what?" he insisted. "Finish what you were saying, Charlott."

Charley glared into Brant's eyes defiantly. "It has just occurred to me that I owe you no explanation," she said adamantly. "As a matter of fact, I owe you nothing at all." One auburn eyebrow arched. "Whatever gave you the idea that I did?"

That stopped him for a moment, but only for a

moment. Reducing the space between them to nothing at all, Brant murmured "this" an instant before he enveloped her body with his arms, and her lips with his mouth.

Yummy! The feel of him, the taste of him, was like chocolate to a chocaholic! Unimportant, the harsh words they'd been slinging at each other mere seconds before; unimportant, the fact that she'd known him little more than twenty-four hours.

Hungrily, greedily, Charley consumed the sweetness of Brant's mouth, moaning a soft protest when he raised his head a fraction of an inch to stare down at her fiercely.

"Sweet Lord!" Brant groaned. "This is all I've been able to think about today! I left my number at least a half dozen times. Why didn't you return my calls?" As if he could not deny himself the pleasure, Brant drew her lower lip inside his mouth, sucking gently as he explored the tender flesh with his tongue. "By midafternoon I'd whipped myself into a frenzy, imagining you doing all kinds of things with all kinds of creeps! And, damn it, it was driving me nuts!"

Without even trying, Brant had managed to insult her twice in less than ten minutes. All kinds of creeps? Creeps! Choked with anger, Charley glared up at him.

"I—I think you had a head start!" she finally sputtered. "I mean as far as being nuts!" She yanked against his hold in an unsuccessful bid to free herself, then went still again. "Brant," she gritted. "Let go of my wrists. If you please," she added bitingly.

"But I don't please," Brant retorted.

"You're hurting me!" Even though it was a lie, Charley thought it was worth a shot.

"I'm not and you know it. But, I admit, the concept is not without appeal."

"Are you saying you get your chuckles from hurting women?" Without reason Charley was positive he did not, yet she couldn't resist the urge to needle him. His soft laughter confirmed her assumption.

"I get my 'chuckles' from a great many things, none of which includes either the giving or receiving of pain." Brant frowned. "That is," he qualified, "I haven't up till now. You, Charlott Marks, activate some very disturbing urges in me."

Charley might have taken a moment to ponder that if he had not begun playing with her lips again. Strangely, wonderfully, though Brant had confessed to harboring dark desires where Charley was concerned, his kiss was heartwrenchingly tender. Releasing his grip on her wrists, he trailed his fingers up the length of her arms. His hands paused at her shoulders to gently knead the tension from her muscles before gliding down her spine as if the cotton gauze were the richest satin.

"Charlott, Charlott." The strangled groan floated to Charley's ears from where Brant's lips now explored the wildly beating pulse in her throat. "I want to make love to you." A shudder trembled through her as the tip of his tongue touched the erratically throbbing vein. "I want to make love *with* you!" Brant corrected himself in a tone strong with conviction.

Yes! Oh, yes! Charley was prevented from sighing the words aloud because Brant's mouth had sought hers again. Pleasurably denied speech as a means of communication, she spoke of her compliance in an ancient, more basic way by curving her softness to the hard contours of his body.

Brant swung her into his arms, his hands possessive as he held her close. He strode across the living room, his mouth still fused to hers, and actually got to within a few feet of her bedroom when the insolent ring of the phone splintered the euphoric haze enveloping Charley's mind.

This time Brant's groan held a different note. "Not again!" His arms tightened. "I don't believe this!" Whether he believed it or not, the ringing persisted.

Her common sense restored, Charley sighed in relief at the intrusion. Incredible as it was, she had again suspended reason while under the spell of Brant's mouth.

"Put me down, Brant, please." Charley's voice, though shaky, held a firm note of command. "I must answer it."

"Why?" Tipping his head, Brant scowled down at her. "Why is it imperative now? The ringing certainly didn't seem to bother you all day."

"Brant." Charley's voice strengthened. "Please put me down."

Very reluctantly Brant set her on her feet, then turned away to stare at the TV, his back rigid. "Make it quick."

Charley might have taken exception to the terse order had it not been issued in a rather ragged tone. She knew how he felt. Wasn't she feeling the same grinding frustration? Oh, she was grateful for the interruption, but that didn't change the fact that her senses still screamed for indulgence. Sighing in despair at her own internal conflict, Charley dashed for the extension phone on a small table at the far end of the couch.

"Did I chase you out of the shower or some other inconvenient place?" Dani laughed at the breathless sound of Charley's voice.

"Oh, hi, Dani!" The beginnings of Charley's smile faded at the sudden taut stillness of Brant's entire length. Had something on the news caught his attention and upset him? Frowning, she dragged her concentration back to her caller. "I was . . . ah . . . occupied." Oh, brother! Charley groaned silently. The understatement of understatements!

"Dare I hope your occupation was with your occupation?" Dani quipped.

This time Charley groaned aloud, then laughed. "Do you ever think of anything else?" Charley teased. "I mean, you really do have a one-track mind!"

"Made me what I am today," Dani drawled. "So, how are you making out with the battle of the brushes? Did you get anything accomplished this afternoon?"

"Yes." Charley lowered her voice. "It was beautiful, Dani, everything clicked. The afternoon simply faded into evening without my noticing. I loved every minute of it." Impossible as it would seem, Brant's long body appeared to tighten even more. Her frown deepening, Charley wondered what could be upsetting about the weather report; surely the good-looking young man who read the report from the weather service had not warned of a monsoon or something equally dire? Charley's attention returned to Dani's insistent voice.

"Did you hear me, Charley?" she asked sharply. "I asked if you were going to get back at it tomorrow?"

"Tomorrow?" Charley repeated vaguely, noting Brant's clenched hands with amazement. What was bugging him? "Not tomorrow, Dani," she decided on the instant. "But soon, I promise."

Dani's sigh was heartfelt. "It's not like you to procrastinate like this, Charley," she scolded gently. "I hope you're not going to suddenly turn temperamental on me?''

Charley laughed softly. ''I wouldn't do that to you, Dani! You know how much I adore you, darling.'' Charley's saccharine tone would have caused envy in the heart of the most famous dramatic actress.

Dani's giggle, so out of character, conveyed her appreciation of Charley's performance. ''Okay,'' she chuckled. ''I get the message. You *are* telling me to mind my own end of the business, are you not?''

''Now you've got the picture.'' Charley laughed with her.

''Not yet,'' Dani retorted. ''But I hope to soon, and not just one either!''

''You don't know when to quit!'' Charley feigned exasperation. ''Good night, Dani, I'll call you Monday.''

Danny, Brant mused. Who the hell was this Danny anyway? Staring blankly at the TV screen, he raked his mind for a face to go with the name; damned if he could think of a Danny among the crowd Charlott ran around with! Of course, rumor had it that she frequently accepted invitations from men outside the ''in'' group, so it wasn't surprising that Brant was unable to pinpoint the man.

While apparently absorbing the weather report, Brant avidly listened to Charlott's end of the conversation, growing more angry by the sentence. Her responses confirmed what he'd suspected: she'd been with a man all day, and that was why she hadn't answered her phone.

Brant knew he should walk out the door, and out of her life, but he couldn't force himself to do it. You are a fool, he told himself scornfully. Charlott Marks is not worth five minutes of your time! Kiss her good-bye and take off. This playground is definitely overcrowded! Brant knew the advice was sound. He also knew he had no intention of heeding it. He *wanted* her more than he'd ever wanted anything before in his adult life. It was almost scary, but there it was. Brant turned around to face her as she replaced the receiver.

"The weather service has predicted a nearly perfect summer day for tomorrow. Come run into the sunshine with me."

Charley knew that if she had her head screwed on correctly, she wouldn't even give consideration to his offhand invitation. But, as she was quickly learning, as far as Brant d'Acier was concerned, her head had definitely been turned! Darn it all, she *wanted* to spend the day with him! And, if she were completely honest with herself, the entire night as well!

"Where would you like to run to?" Charley really didn't care about his destination as much as she wanted to avoid her own thoughts.

"Wherever." His shoulders rippled in a shrug. "There are certainly plenty of interesting sights around here to investigate." He smiled with beguiling sweetness, robbing Charley of breath for a moment. "Plenty of historical ones too. We can learn something while enjoying the outing."

Not to mention the possibility of gleaning some ideas for future paintings, Charley concluded privately. Grasping at research as an excuse, she tossed caution to the wind. "A trip into history will snare me every time." Charley smiled back at him. "What time will you pick me up?"

"Are you a late sleeper on Sunday?"

"Usually," she admitted without embarrassment. "But for special outings I make an exception."

"Then I'll be sure to make this outing very special," Brant promised. "Will eight be too early?"

Charley pretended to give grave consideration to the question. Then, mocking him with her eyes and smile, she voiced her one and only condition. "No . . . that is if you leave right away so I can get my beauty rest." Her expression impish, she waited for the usual compliment. But Brant let his opinion of her beauty blaze in the brilliant gaze he swept over her slender form. The smile that feathered his lips said volumes about his appreciation of her attractiveness.

Transfixed by Brant's hot gaze, Charley stared at him helplessly for long moments, practically begging him to take her into his arms. Accurately interpreting her look, Brant walked slowly to where she was curled into the corner of the couch. His movement brought Charley to her senses. Was she mad? she berated herself. She was playing with dynamite here!

"I said right away!" Laughing softly, Charley slipped off the couch, deftly eluding the large hands that reached out to impede her escape. Safely positioned at the door, she raised one brow. "It's almost midnight, Brant. If you are not out of here by the stroke of twelve, I may be forced to cancel our day in the sunshine."

Acknowledging defeat with a grin, Brant strolled to her. "It seems round two is yours also." Swiftly dipping his head, he planted a hard kiss on her lips but moved away the instant he felt her respond. "But," he drawled, turning to open the door, "as this is beginning to look like a championship fight, my rounds will come." Brant stepped into the hallway before firing his parting shot. ''I'll have you on the mat long before the bell sounds on round fifteen.'' Exuding confidence, he sauntered down the hall, calling back ''eight o'clock'' as he entered the elevator.

Leaning against the door, Charley allowed her satisfaction full rein. Oh, she was looking forward to round three! Brant was dangerous, yes, but he was fun as well; much more fun than the boring, predictable men she'd gone out with up till now.

Smiling dreamily, Charley ambled to the couch and curled up in the corner before lifting her forgotten glass of wine. Sipping daintily, she replayed the previous hour in her mind, her eyes sparkling when she recalled the way the evening had ended.

Poor Brant, she mused, how frustrating to have his intentions thwarted by interruptions two nights running! Laughter bubbled in Charley's throat, then was choked off as she sat up abruptly, cradling her glass in her palms to prevent the wine from spilling over. How perfect! How absolutely perfect! Poor Brant, indeed!

Swinging her legs to the floor, Charley carefully set her glass on the coffee table. Laughing aloud, she actually rubbed her hands together as she plotted future frustrations for Brant d'Acier. The plan forming in her mind was delightful in its simplicity. All she had to do to keep him in line was to arrange interruptions whenever she even suspected they might be alone together. The plan had its drawbacks, of course; there were bound to be times when she would accidentally find herself alone with him. But, if she kept her wits about her, and her emotions under control, she should be able to limit the number of those times.

Feeling not a twinge of guilt for her deviousness, Charley picked up her glass and swallowed a mouthful of the dry wine. All's fair in love and war, she assured herself. And in the male-female game of cat and mouse, surely the mouse, lacking superior strength, was allowed intellectual maneuvers?

Uncoiling her long legs, Charley rose slowly. She slid her hands under and up through her tangled mass of hair as she stretched luxuriously. A smile twitched at the corners of her mouth while she strolled into the kitchen to pour the remainder of her wine down the drain before rinsing the delicate stemmed glass and placing it carefully on the dish rack. After switching off the lights she drifted into the bedroom, positive she'd have no trouble sleeping. Her assumption proved correct; Charley was lost to reality within minutes of the time her body hit the pastel-colored sheets.

Damn! Was he to endure another sleepless night?

Sighing in disgust, Brant changed position for what seemed like the hundredth time since he'd gone to bed over two hours earlier.

"You know how much I adore you, darling."

Brant gritted his teeth as the softly voiced assurance repeated itself like a litany in his mind. Who the hell was this Danny? What kind of bedroom games was Charley playing, and with how many different men?

Worst of all, she had denied *him* again.

Brant's thoughts, usually clear and precise, swirled around without making any sense of the problem. And always they returned to that one ego-deflating fact.

She had denied him again.

For Brant, sleep was a long time arriving.

Chapter Five

For the second morning in a row Charley was awakened by the shrill summons of the telephone; this time she answered it.

"Why didn't you return my calls, Red?" It was the aggrieved voice of her current gallant.

Charley was immediately sorry she'd taken the call. Today was her day in the sunshine with Brant! The last thing she felt like doing was soothing Luther Holtzman's ruffled feathers.

"I was simply too tired to bother myself with returning *all* my calls by the time I fell into bed last night, Luther," Charley lied lazily. "Was there something important you wanted to talk about?" she inquired in a sweet if obviously bored tone.

"Whom were you out with?" came the predictable query.

Charley sighed loudly. Lou knew too well what her reply would be. How many times had they enacted this particular scene? "I hardly think that is any of your business, Lou." Now he would say he wanted to make every facet of her life his business.

Lou did not disappoint her. "I want to make everything about you my business. I want to make *you* my business. You know how I feel about you, Charley!"

Oh, yes, I know! Charley grimaced. I know that you believe that every one of your friends has been in my bed at one time or another, and you're ticked off because you haven't! "You love me?" she asked in a sugary voice.

"Of course I love you! You know I love you!"

I know that, like every one of your ilk, you believe that saying those magic words will gain you entrance into my bed! Charley did not speak her bitter thoughts aloud. What a shame, she mused. Luther Holtzman was an attractive, wealthy young man. He'd be a terrific catch for some equally attractive, wealthy young woman. But not for her, Charley vowed. She had no use whatever for the males in good standing with the monied crowd, the females either, come to that!

"Are you still there, Red?" Lou demanded when she was quiet too long.

That was another point against him; Charley loathed the nickname "Red." "Yes, Lou, I'm still here. But not for long. I have a date." Let him chew on that bit of information.

Lou didn't chew very long. In fact, he spit out his annoyance at once. "A date? Whom with?"

"A deliciously handsome devil," she told him with relish. Yet another of the top-drawer bunch with designs on my virtue, she added to herself with equal relish. A high flyer about to be shot down! "We're going to steep ourselves in history."

"Sounds pretty dull to me," Lou grumbled.

It would, since you have a one-track mind! "Did you have a reason for calling so early in the morning?" Charley asked, letting her tone convey growing impatience.

Lou's sigh was designed to break a lady's heart but, as Charley was the very last person to think of herself as a lady, her heart remained unbroken.

"Lou, really!" Charley was fed up with his dramatics. "I've got to get ready to go. Could you please tell me why you called?"

"All right," Lou relented. "I called to invite you to go to a party on Wednesday evening."

Not *another* party! Charley swallowed an indelicate snort of impatience. This had to be the seventh party invitation she'd received since the beginning of the month, and the month was not yet half over. How utterly boring! Lou must have decided she was on the point of refusing—which she was—because he rushed on. "Please say you'll come, darling. All our friends will be there."

Yet another reason to refuse, Charley thought wryly. She opened her mouth to do so, but again Lou spoke first.

"The party's being given by Louis d'Acier. Do you know him?"

I know his son much better! At least I know he's a very physical man! Smiling at her assessment of Brant, Charley said offhandedly, "I met him at the award dinner Friday night. He seems very nice."

Encouraged by her remark, Lou agreed eagerly, "Oh, he is. And he's got more connections than the telephone company!"

Charley made a face at the phone; there speaks the true social climber. No matter what rung he was at, Lou yearned to go higher.

"Will you come, darling?"

"Yes," Charley murmured, thinking that this party fit in perfectly with her schemes. "What time is the party?"

"Early. It's to be an outside bash with a buffet supper. Oh, and bring your swim suit, I hear he's got an enormous pool."

Charley suffered a few more minutes of Lou's "darlings" before she finally convinced him she had to hang up. Then, pressed for time, she decided to forgo breakfast in the interest of looking as ravishing as possible.

Brant's expression when she opened the door assured Charley that her fast had not been in vain. Still, she could not repress the tiny growl of hunger her stomach emitted.

"Hungry?" Brant asked with a grin.

"Starving," Charley admitted, grinning back. "I didn't take time to eat breakfast."

"Neither did I, and I'm starving too." Stepping back into the hall, Brant held his hand out invitingly. "Shall we start the day by gorging ourselves?"

After locking the door behind her, Charley slipped her hand into his. "I'd love to begin by gorging." She laughed up at him.

"Then I'm afraid you'll have to make do with a cup of coffee and a thin slice of toast for a few hours." At her quizzically arched brow he explained. "There's a restaurant on 202 near Brandywine that is very popular for its Sunday buffets. The problem, as far as we're concerned, is that they don't open until ten-thirty. Can you hold out until then?''

"Only if you feed me the toast and coffee immediately," Charley warned, only half jokingly.

Over steaming coffee and pieces of toast, Brant gave Charley a rundown of their itinerary for the day.

"I thought we'd begin by exploring Fairmount Park. We could stroll a bit, check out the mansions—Strawberry, Sweetbriar, Lemon Hill. We probably won't be able to see half the attractions before it's time to head toward Brandywine and breakfast, but''—he shrugged—''we can only do so much in one day.''

"How true," Charley agreed laughingly.

"Since we'll be in the neighborhood," Brant went on, "we may as well take in the Brandywine River Museum too.''

Suddenly fully alert, Charley asked carefully, "You're into art?''

"In most of its forms." Brant studied her intently. "Why? Does it leave you cold?''

"No. Would it matter to you if it did?''

Brant favored her with a sardonic smile. "Don't play coy, Charlott. You know very well I'd agree to a change of plans if I thought you'd be bored.''

"I will not be bored." Afraid of showing too much enthusiasm, Charley kept her tone bland. "Frankly, I rather like N. C. Wyeth's work.''

"Good." Brant finished the last of his coffee. "The museum stands.''

"I sincerely hope so." Charley's dry retort gained her a genuine smile from Brant. "And after the museum?''

Brant's eyes gleamed with the deviltry Charley was becoming familiar with. "I'll tell you that after we've gorged on food and masterpieces."

They followed Brant's itinerary to the letter, traipsing around the park like a couple of teenagers out on a lark. They admired the mansions, stood on the bank of the Schuykill River to watch the scull crews work out, and drank in the serenity of the exquisite Japanese garden. Before heading for Brandywine, they lingered awhile in the Philadelphia Museum of Art, each admitting that the famous museum was a favorite haunt.

They didn't arrive at the restaurant until after eleven, and then they had to wait to be seated. By the time their waitress invited them to help themselves to the buffet tables, the delicious aromas wafting through the large establishment had them both ravenous.

Over crab omelets, succulent slices of ham, fresh fruit, and croissants, Brant brought up the subject of Louis d'Acier's party.

"My father is having some friends to the house Wednesday evening. I was wondering if you'd like to come?" He paused but not long enough for Charley to speak. "Your father will be there," he added, as if that might be an inducement.

"Really?" Charley made no attempt to hide her surprise. "My father rarely attends parties."

"I know." Brant's smile conveyed understanding. "Since they began working together on the design of the house, your father and mine have become good friends." He raised one dark brow. "But that doesn't answer the question. Will you go with me?"

Disappointment stabbed at Charley, shocking her with its intensity. It's only a party, she told herself. And you don't even *like* parties! Her defenses restored, Charley shook her head gently. "I'm sorry, but I've already accepted an invitation to your father's party."

"From whom?"

The sharpness of Brant's tone might have angered Charley if it hadn't pleased her so much. "An old friend," she answered simply.

Brant's gaze narrowed on her face. "How old? And how friendly?"

Now Charley did feel a twinge of anger; she allowed no one the right to question her personal life. Straightening her spine, she gave him her most haughty look. "As to who he is, you'll find that out on Wednesday evening. As to how friendly he is, that is none of your business." Relaxing against the back of her chair, Charley waited for Brant's response, hoping, yet afraid to hope, that he would not turn out to be as dully predictable as all the other men she'd ever met. Not once did she wonder why she longed for him to be different.

Brant did not rush to protest, and in that alone he proved different. Taking his time, sipping his coffee, he studied her withdrawn expression thoughtfully for several minutes. "You're right," he agreed, to her surprise. "It is none of my business. Forget I asked." Tipping his cup, he drained it, then set it down decisively. "Are you ready for the museum?"

Oddly, Charley felt slighted; Brant hadn't had to be that different! Rats! What *was* the matter with her anyway? It wasn't as if Brant *meant* anything to her other than playing cat to her mouse in their little game. Get it together, girl, she advised herself, managing a carefree smile. "Ready for anything," she assured him brightly.

"Anything?" Brant slanted her a wicked glance. "I

can imagine some very interesting 'anythings.' Dare I
hope you're ready for all of them?''

"I think not!" Fighting laughter, Charley contrived a
prim façade. It wasn't easy; this was the first man ever
who could truly amuse her!

"I was afraid you'd say that." Brant sighed. "Oh,
well, shall we go wallow in culture instead?''

Although they did not exactly wallow, Charley mused
later, they did view a good number of the impressive
offerings of the Brandywine colony artists. An added
bonus was the view of the surrounding countryside from
the all-glass towers of the converted mill in which the
museum was housed.

While perusing the paintings, Charley remained silent
for the most part, listening intently to Brant's opinions.
To her amazement his observations were concise and
astute, and she found herself forming a respect for his
artistic taste.

"You really are into art, aren't you?" she remarked at
one point.

"I'm afraid I must fall back on the standard response
to that question." Brant smiled. "I know what I like."
His gaze settled on a seascape hung nearby.

Watching him, Charley had the impression that he was
not really seeing the canvas but contemplating instead
some inner vision. "Do you like that one?" she asked
gently, her gaze shifting to the well-executed study of a
summer bright beach awash with foamy ocean wavelets.

"Hmmm? Oh, yes." A small smile curving his lips,
Brant focused on the painting. "It's very good, but
actually I wasn't really looking at it. I was seeing
another, quite different seascape, very moody, turbulent, haunting." Moving sharply, he swung around to

face her. "I saw it at a Max Charles showing. I tried to buy it, but I'd arrived at the gallery late and I was told it had already been sold. I never even found out who'd purchased it."

I know where it is. Becoming perfectly still, Charley tightened her lips to keep from blurting out the information. What possible purpose would it serve to tell him the Charles seascape was very close by, in the possession of a young journalist named Paige Prescott, who lived only a few miles away in Chadds Ford? *None whatever,* Charley answered herself. Not only would it serve no purpose, it could very well cause problems. If Brant became curious as to how she'd garnered the information, then began to probe . . . Charley strengthened her resolve to remain silent. The quiet sound of his voice drew her from introspection.

"Although I like many current artists, I am especially partial to the work of Max Charles." Brant shrugged lightly. "I'm not quite sure how to explain it, but there's an indefinable quality about the man's paintings that speaks to me." He smiled wryly. "Do you have any idea what I'm talking about? Are you even familiar with his work?"

How in the world was she to respond to his questions? Charley certainly was not about to confess that she *was* Max Charles! Less than a half dozen people were privy to that information! Still, she had to give him some sort of answer. Of course, his second question was easy. "Yes," Charley replied somberly. "I'm familiar with Max Charles's work." Oh, brother, was she ever familiar! There were days, weeks when all she could think of was completing a Max Charles piece! "And I think I understand what you're talking about." "Curious," she murmured, "What is the first thing you think when viewing a Charles painting?"

"The first thing . . ." Brant frowned in concentration.

Charley was immediately sorry she'd asked his opinion. She was sure his answer would disappoint her; she had stopped asking the question long ago simply because the responses, though varied, always disappointed her. Oh, there were those rare individuals, like Paige Prescott, who understood the essence of her work, but they were few and far between.

"Strength."

Charley was electrified! No one else had ever described the essence of what she strove for so concisely. Experiencing a sensation strangely akin to fear, Charley stared up into his thoughtful eyes and slowly took one step back.

"Haven't you seen it in his work?" Brant smiled. "I mean, I don't see how anybody could miss it. I think I've seen most of his paintings, and it's in all of them—that declaration of sheer strength."

"Really?" Charley returned his smile weakly. "I . . . ah . . . never thought about it." Get off the subject! The command exploded in her mind. At least until you can think about it objectively, adjust to this unexpected sensitivity of his. Charley avoided the intensity of their discussion by stepping back into the role of superficial social butterfly. "All I know is, with each successive showing Charles's work commands a higher price and—"

"I know," Brant interrupted harshly. "You have a taste for rich things." All the warmth in him fled. "Do you own a Max Charles original?"

"Certainly." Charley's flip reply concealed a growing pain in her chest. "I own . . . several." Actually her studio was lined with early works that she would not allow to be shown.

Brant's features tightened into a mask of anger. His hard, proud jaw jutted forward; his beautiful cheekbones seemed even more prominent. Dark eyes, savage with anger, stared at her down the length of his long, chiseled nose. If Brant intended the look to be intimidating, he was successful. "And did Stephen sign his name to the checks that covered the exorbitant amount required to purchase those 'several' originals?" he gritted.

"My father?" The pain inside threatened to close her throat. Hanging on to the role she'd so carefully fashioned to protect herself from the prying eyes of society, Charley raised her brows mockingly. "Of course not! I . . . procured . . . them for myself." Charley used the word *procured* deliberately.

Brant recoiled as if she'd suddenly grown horns. Spinning on his heel, he strode away from her, snarling, "Let's get out of here! I've lost my appetite for art."

Trying to appear nonchalant, Charley sauntered after Brant, wondering sadly if she had finally succeeded in alienating him completely. What had happened to the game? What had happened to her plan to amuse herself with him? What was happening to *her?* Unprepared to face the answers to those questions, Charley pushed conjecture away by addressing Brant.

"Would you consider it impertinent if I ask where we are going?"

The look Brant turned on her stopped Charley in her tracks. It spoke of dislike, and disgust, and, chillingly, an unwanted yet compulsive desire. The look said I want you, and I hate both of us for it.

Shivering in the balmy air of the summer day, Charley bit back a cry of protest, unaware that her eyes betrayed the pain he was causing her. All she knew was that the fire in Brant's eyes was suddenly extinguished and he looked as exhausted as she felt.

"The day's losing its warmth." Brant's flat observation had nothing to do with the weather, and Charley knew it. "I had planned to spend the rest of the afternoon touring the usual attractions, Independence Hall, the Betsy Ross House, and so forth, then wind up the day with dinner at Bookbinder's." His recital was less than enthusiastic. "Do you want to complete this marathon tour?"

Perversely his disinterest provoked a reaction in Charley. She could handle his disapproval. She could even deal with his disgust. But in no way could she remain nonchalant in the face of his disinterest.

"Why not? It sure has been a barrel of laughs so far."

"And entertainment comes right after expensive things on your list of priorities," Brant shot back. "Doesn't it?"

"Yes, of course." Breezing by him, Charley walked to the car and stood tapping the sole of her sandal impatiently on the ground. In truth, Charley wanted desperately to go home, lock herself in, and have a good cry. Cry? Over a man? Ridiculous! Hadn't she promised herself long ago that she would never again shed tears over a man? She had. Yet, here she was, feeling positively weepy.

"I'm sorry." There was a note of contrition in Brant's

low voice, and she blinked furiously against the tears in her eyes.

"I have no right to pass judgment on your priorities, your lifestyle, or anything else." Brant had come up to stand behind her, now he moved to face her. "You confuse me, Charlott, and I don't like being confused." A sad smile touched his lips fleetingly. "Have I ruined our day?"

Charley shook her head before slowly raising her eyes to his. There was a smile on his face, a smile so tender, so gentle, that it caused a lump in her throat. That smile was her undoing. Charley knew she had to face a few hard facts. From their first meeting she had deliberately misled him, goaded him, teased him. What right did she have to get angry when he retaliated? Brant had been honest with her from the beginning. Now she owed him a little honesty.

"I'm sorry too, Brant." Her smile was shaky. "And if the day has been ruined, it's because of me, not you. I invited your criticism by needling you." Charley lifted her shoulders, then dropped them again. "I'll understand if you take me directly home"—her smile grew wry—"then run for the hills."

"Are you suggesting I desert the field of battle?" Brant teased. "Do I look like a quitter?"

Charley laughed. "A quitter? You? Spare me the dramatics!" Encouraged by his answering grin, she asked hopefully, "Are you saying you're not taking me home?"

Brant took the time to insert the key in the lock and swing the passenger door open before replying. "That's exactly what I'm saying. Slide in . . . if you can take the heat."

Fully aware of the double meaning in his words, Charley slid onto the seat and stifled a yelp when her thighs touched the hot leather. The inside of the car was airless, the seat blazingly hot. Raising her hips, Charley smoothed her lightweight cotton skirt down, then gingerly resettled herself. "I knew I should have worn slacks," she muttered.

"And cover up those gorgeous legs?" Brant exclaimed. "I'm delighted you decided on that little dress!"

That "little" dress had carried an astronomical price tag! True, the top consisted of only a loose bodice and two thin shoulder straps, and there was not an awful lot to the skirt, but the material was of the finest cotton, and the blending shades of muted green and white were delightfully cool looking. Thrilling to the appreciation gleaming in Brant's eyes, Charley was suddenly very grateful for the urge that had driven her to splurge on the garment.

"Ah . . ." Charley had to pause to wet her lips. "It's getting late. If we don't make a move soon, we'll never get back to town before Independence Hall and the Betsy Ross House close for the day."

"I was thinking about making a move." Brant laughed softly. "But not necessarily in the direction of town." He sighed exaggeratedly. "Oh, well, this was my idea, wasn't it?"

"It was, sir." Charley spoiled the effect of her prim tone by fluttering her lashes outrageously. "I think the word you used was *marathon*."

Brant shot a quick glance at the slim gold watch encircling his wrist. "I'm afraid that is exactly what it will turn out to be." Handling the big car with ease, he drove through the parking lot and onto the highway. "Even if I break the speed limit, we'll be cutting it close." His gaze left the road to glance at her. "I'll leave it to you. We can rush through the rest of the tour, or leave it for another day and go on to dinner."

Charley grinned. "If it's all the same to you, I'd just as soon go on to dinner. Even though I've been to the historical sites many times, I have a tendency to dawdle exactly like a tourist, oohing and aahing over everything."

"Ah-ha," Brant said eagerly. "Do I detect another American history buff?"

"Another?"

"I'm a pushover concerning anything that has to do with the making of this country in general, and Philadelphia in particular." Unlike many people Charley could think of, Brant displayed no embarrassment at admitting he loved his country. "And, like you, I have a tendency to dawdle whenever I tour. Okay, dinner it is, although we will be a little early for our reservation."

Charley frowned in perplexity. "When did you make reservations?"

"During brunch, when I left the table to go to the men's room," Brant said smugly. "Had you thought you were dealing with a dummy?"

"Not very likely," Charley retorted. "Had you?"

"Not very likely," Brant mimicked. "My daddy didn't raise any fools!"

They were early for their reservation so, at Brant's request, they were shown into the President's Bar. There, they sipped their margaritas and admired the impressive array of portraits.

"You know, this bar was brought here from a ghost

town,'' Brant informed her, rubbing his hand lightly over the beautiful mahogany finish. ''Elko, Nevada, to be exact.''

''Really?'' Charley asked, keeping her face straight with effort; she didn't have the heart to tell him she knew where the bar came from. He seemed to be having such a good time educating her.

Brant's wry smile told her he'd seen through her act. ''Am I beginning to sound pompous?''

''Not at all!'' Charley objected. ''You sound . . . well, rather proud of the fact that it's here.''

''Oddly, I am.'' Brant chuckled. ''You'd think I personally lugged the thing across country on my back!''

''But isn't that good?'' Charley frowned in concentration. ''I mean, having the ability to get so wrapped up in our history that you can project yourself into it?'' Her frown gave way to a smile. ''Does that make any sense at all?''

''It makes a good deal of sense, at least to me.'' Brant grinned. ''But then, I'm—''

Charley was not destined to learn what Brant was, for at that moment he was interrupted by the hostess informing him that their table was ready. Following the trim woman, Charley sighed in pleasure at the realization that they would be seated in the famous main dining room. Her pleasure deepened when they were shown to a table near the great fireplace, built of cobblestones worn smooth by the tramp of British and American soldiers and flanked by cannons from the Revolutionary war.

Along with tender broiled scallops and garden fresh vegetables, Charley and Brant sipped chilled white wine and immersed themselves in history—each other's.

Chapter Six

"What do you mean, you're not into Mohegan tradition?" Charley exclaimed in disbelief.

"Oh, I know the basics, of course," Brant explained easily, unperturbed by her shocked expression. "The same as I know the basics of my French heritage. For instance, I know that I was named for the Mohawk fighter and later missionary, Joseph Brant or Thayendanegea. I also know the surname d'Acier means man of steel. I have a loose knowledge of both sides of my ancestry, but that's about it." Brant shrugged. "Were you aware that my mother was from Canada?"

"No." Fascinated by even this tiny bit of information about him, Charley asked, "Is her birthplace important?"

"In this case, yes." Brant paused to refill their glasses. "You see, when my mother, a full-blooded

Indian, married my father, a non-Indian, she lost her Indian status automatically, and so did I.''

"You're kidding!''

"Not at all,'' Brant assured her. "But don't let it upset you. I consider myself neither an Indian nor a Frenchman. I consider myself an American.''

"Still—'' Charley got no further, for Brant smoothly interrupted her.

"Enough about me. What about you?''

"Me!'' Charley snorted. "Nothing very exciting about my history. I come from good, common German stock. As far as I know, my ancestors have been in this area since day one.'' She grinned. "Well, maybe day two.''

"And that red mop of yours?'' Brant asked dryly.

"There are no redheaded Germans?'' Charley asked, managing to look amazed. When Brant raised a dark brow skeptically, she laughingly confessed, "Okay, my maternal grandmother came directly from the 'old sod.' Her name was Pegeen, and she was a flaming redhead. My mother always maintained that I was the mirror image of Pegeen.''

"And are you?'' Brant asked.

"Beats me.'' Charley shrugged. "If there were ever any pictures of her, they got lost in the shuffle along the way. She died when my mother was twelve, trying, for the fifth time, to give my grandfather a son.''

Relaxing against the back of his chair to allow the waiter to clear the table, Brant drank the last of his wine, studying her thoughtfully over the rim of the fragile glass. After ordering coffee and declining dessert for both of them, he probed gently, "Did I detect a hint of bitterness in your tone in reference to your grandfather?''

''A little, perhaps,'' Charley conceded. ''Though he had four daughters, my grandfather insisted on a son, even after the doctor had warned him that another pregnancy would very likely kill his wife.'' Charley's smile held sad remembrance. ''My mother told me Pegeen was beautiful, and talented, and loving. She loved her husband and wanted to please him; she died in the process.'' Charley's sigh was more heartfelt than Brant could possibly know. Pegeen had been an artist. ''I would have loved to know Pegeen.''

Shaking off her momentary sadness, Charley smiled at the waiter as he served their coffee. ''On to my father,'' she continued lightly when the waiter moved away. ''Dad's parents were both hearty Germans.'' She smiled conspiratorially, as if imparting a secret. ''My father is brilliant, you know.''

''Yes,'' Brant answered simply, seriously. ''I've known for some time.''

Not again! First astute artistic judgment. Then emotional sensitivity. Now Brant had displayed intellectual discernment. It wasn't fair! He wasn't supposed to be this way!

''Does that surprise you?'' Brant asked.

She nodded. ''For years no one recognized his abilities. Now, of course, he's been proclaimed an overnight success.''

''You resent it, don't you?'' Brant observed. ''This overnight success that was twenty years in the making?'' His compassionate smile killed the last of her preconceived ideas of his character. ''Of course you do,'' he answered for her. "You'd be less than human if you didn't."

Suddenly Charley was scared. This man threatened her in a way that was infinitely more frightening than the fear of a physical attack; this man was a threat to her mind!

"Charlott, talk to me about it," Brant coaxed softly.

She didn't want to talk about it. Not now. It was too late for talk, ten years of bitterness too late. She had spent too much time harboring the resentment in her heart, too much time cultivating it into an integral element of her "self."

I want to go home!

It was more than a thought, more than a silent cry, more than an inward plea; it was an all-encompassing knowledge of what she had to do for the preservation of the person inside the persona.

"I would like to go home now, please."

"I don't understand you!" Brant frowned.

Good! Her façade securely in place, Charley lowered her lashes with a long, fluttering sweep. "What's to understand? It's been a long day. To borrow your own expression, a marathon. I've been entertained and well fed. Now all I want to do is kick my shoes off and relax. Please, Brant. I don't want to talk; I want to go home."

"All right." His movements abrupt, Brant slipped his wallet from the back pocket of the casual slacks. Extracting several bills, he laid them atop the check then circled her chair to pull it out while she rose. "I'll kick off my shoes, too, and relax with you." Brant's breath caressed her cheek as he politely grasped her elbow to escort her from the dining room.

"Brant." Charley kept her voice low to avoid undue attention as they made their way through the restaurant, but it held a warning just the same. "I was not issuing an invitation. I said I do not want to talk."

"Okay," he agreed far too easily. Stepping in front of her, he held the door for her. A complacent smile was on his lips.

Her suspicion aroused, Charley cast him a narrow-eyed glance as she preceded him out of the building. Her suspicions were confirmed as he followed her toward the car.

"We won't talk," he promised softly. "We'll make love instead."

"We'll do no such thing!" Charley gasped indignantly, swinging around to face him. Looking at him was a mistake. Lord, he was sexy! Lit by the late lingering sunlight, Brant's eyes appeared fired by a flame from deep within. Charley actually took a step toward him before coming to her senses.

Was she out of her mind? They were standing less than ten feet from the entrance to the restaurant; people were circling around them, giving them curious looks, coming and going. Yet, there they both stood, gazing into each other's eyes as if mesmerized. It was not until she tried to speak that Charley realized she was holding her breath . . . or had Brant stolen it? At that moment she derived little consolation from the realization that Brant had stopped breathing too. Raking her mind for a cutting put-down, Charley grasped at the first idea that drifted into her consciousness.

"A day of sightseeing and dinner, even at the famous Bookbinder's, hardly comes under the heading of *everything*." Flicking her hair off her shoulders with an

arrogant toss of her head, Charley shattered the illusion
of intimacy. She drew herself to her full height and said
coolly, "I don't think you can afford me, Mr. d'Acier."
And I know I can't afford you, she added to herself,
deliberately turning her back and walking briskly to the
big car.

"How could you know whether I can afford you or
not?" Brant growled angrily. He held the door for her
and slammed it after her. *"Everything. The earth,"* he
recited, sliding behind the wheel. He sat rigidly still for a
minute, then thrust the key into the ignition and twisted
it violently. "What the hell does that mean?" he snarled,
slowly weaving the car through the lot to gain access to
the street. "Quote me a concrete figure, and *I'll* decide
whether or not I can afford it."

Fool, fool, fool, Charley berated herself. Did you
really think a man like Brant would be satisfied with such
an ambiguous answer? With vivid clarity her father's
warning rang in her ears: *If you fool around with Brant
d'Acier, you are going to get hurt.* And, sure enough,
here she was, less than forty-eight hours later, hurting
something fierce.

Gazing out of the side window at the twilit streets,
Charley sighed when she realized why she was hurting.
Brant might be more astute, more sensitive, and more
intelligent than all the other men she knew but, in the
final analysis, he was exactly the same as they. He
thought he could buy her with *things*.

How confused can one woman's thinking get? Charley
wondered wryly. She hadn't wanted him to prove
himself different, had she? No, of course she hadn't! So,
then, why was she miserable now that he'd proved he
was the same as all the rest? Circles within circles.

Charley was dizzying herself with her own circular logic. Where, or when, had she lost sight of her original goal—that of leading Brant a merry chase?

"Can't you decide what you want most?"

Charley was so deep into her convoluted thinking process, she started at the sarcastic question from the man beside her. She breathed deeply before turning to look at his rigid profile. "Oh, I know exactly what I want, Mr. d'Acier." At least I used to, she amended silently.

When she again lapsed into silence, Brant sighed roughly. "Well? Are you going to tell me what it is, or am I supposed to guess?"

Charley's burst of laughter was short and strained. "I doubt very much that you could ever guess correctly, Mr. d'Acier."

"Damn it, Charlott!" Brant exploded. "If you call me Mr. d'Acier one more time, I swear I'll stop the car and . . . and . . ."

"Beat me?" Charley supplied sweetly.

"Kiss you," Brant corrected her every bit as sweetly. "I do not get my kicks from manhandling women." His smile flashed briefly. "Not when there's a much more satisfying form of punishment to inflict."

Punishment? Charley gulped back a groan. She had tasted his form of punishment on the two previous evenings. Merely thinking about it made her blood run hot!

"I'm waiting, Charlott," Brant said flatly. "What do you want?"

How could she answer? What could she say? Brant honestly believed she was available to the highest bidder. Glancing out the window, Charley sighed, partly in relief, partly in despair. Relief because they were almost at her apartment, despair because she had given Brant cause for his belief.

"I'll think about it and let you know," she promised in desperation.

"Think about it?" Brant exclaimed as he drove into the parking area. "Damn it, Charlott! You just told me you know exactly what you want!"

Grasping the door handle in order to make a quick getaway, Charley raked her mind for an out. "Oh, I do," she assured him, swinging the door open as he brought the car to a stop. "But what I have to consider is what I want *first*." She twisted around to face him. "Don't get out, please. It's not necessary."

"Charlott—" Brant began.

"Please, Brant, not tonight," Charley interrupted urgently. "I really am tired. I had a lovely day but . . ."

"But you don't want to extend it into a lovely evening," Brant finished for her. Even as he spoke, his hand shot out to curl around the back of her neck, twisting her body even more as he hauled her across the seat to him.

"If you think you're getting out of this car without kissing me, you're crazy," he muttered, capturing the lips she'd parted to protest his treatment.

Sweet, sweet punishment! The thought drifted through Charley. Then, abandoning all reason, she gave herself up to the ravishment of Brant's hungry mouth, moaning softly when his tongue thrust boldly between her lips. By the time he released his hold on her mouth Charley was practically begging for more.

"You see how it is with us?" Brant growled into her ear. "I need you so badly, I've got the shakes, and I can feel the need in you too." He cupped her face with his palm. "Charlott," he whispered urgently. "We are both mature adults. What are we doing sitting in this damn car? We are long past the hurried petting of the teenage stage. Invite me in."

Shrugging free of his light hold, Charley leaned back, away from the enticement of his lips. "No, Brant." She shook her head to reinforce her denial. "Not tonight."

"When? Do I have to make an appointment? Is that it?" Although he kept his voice pitched low, there was a savage undertone to it that sent an apprehensive thrill down Charley's spine. "Do you make love by appointment only?"

"Brant!" Feeling wounded, Charley stared at Brant. A surge of anger saved her from humiliating tears. Damn it! What Brant thought was one thing, what he said to her was something else altogether! "You have no right to talk to me like that! And, if I *did* dispense favors by appointment, *you* would be the last person I'd grant one to." Backing along the seat, she again tried to escape, only to be halted by his hand grasping her upper arm.

"Charlott, wait!"

"No!" Charley had heard just about enough. "Good night—no, good-bye, Mr. d'Acier!" Freeing herself with a violent jerk of her arm, she jumped from the car and ran to the safety of the apartment building, ignoring the sound of Brant calling her name.

Charley did not breathe deeply until she was inside her apartment, with the doors securely locked behind her. She crossed the room on unsteady legs and dropped onto the first chair she came to. Curling into a ball of misery, she rested her head on the chair's broad arm.

I won't cry. I will not cry. Oh, nuts! I'll cry if I want to! Sniffing loudly in the quiet room, Charley gave up the argument and let the hot tears flow freely. That . . . that arrogant blueblood! How dare he speak to me as if I were dirt beneath his feet! Will you never learn, Charlott Marks? she upbraided herself, swiping ineffectually at the tears scalding her cheeks. How many times must you be put down before you learn to guard your defenses more carefully? You left yourself wide open for this one. You knew better; still, you had to have a little fun by indulging yourself at his expense. If you are hurting now, you have only yourself to blame.

Brant d'Acier was honest in his approach, Charley admitted to herself, blatant, but honest. He had stated his intentions less than ten minutes after meeting her. If there were a deceiver in this farce, it was she, Charley acknowledged guiltily, hiccuping a little sob. But, damn him, did Brant have to be so very cruel?

Let her go.

Brant slid between the sheets on his huge bed and realized that suddenly it seemed very empty. Why the bed should seem so empty all of a sudden was cause for some consternation; Brant had never brought a woman to this bed.

Frowning in the darkness, Brant quizzed himself as to the reason he'd never invited a woman into this particular bed. He certainly hadn't hesitated about sharing his bed in the apartment he'd occupied before buying this house two years ago. Not that there'd been all that many women; there had not. A sardonic smile twisted Brant's lips. At least there had not been as many as he'd been credited with! Even so, there had been some, but not in this house, and never in this bed.

Why? Brant's frown deepened as he explored his own motives. What was so special about this place? Stretching out a long arm, he smoothed his palm over the wide expanse of cool sheet next to him. Why was he saving that place? And for whom?

Let her go.

Again the errant thought drifted into Brant's mind. But why now, at this moment? Distractedly his hand again swept the sheet beside his taut body, and a vision of Charlott's face, laughing up at him as they'd strolled the Fairmount Park grounds, imprinted itself on the inside of Brant's closed eyelids. She is so very beautiful, he mused. So very delicate in appearance, so very amoral. Grimacing, Brant endured the shudder that racked his taut body. God, I need her!

Let her go.

I cannot. Sighing softly, defeatedly, Brant deliberately conjured Charlott's image. By running the tip of his tongue over his bottom lip, he stirred the memory of the taste of her provocative mouth. Flexing his fingers, he imagined he could feel the silkiness of her skin. This time Brant's sigh came from the depths of his being. He didn't like the feeling, but fighting it would prove nothing. He wanted her, he needed her, perhaps more than he'd ever wanted or needed anything in his life. Brant's fingers gripped the sheet spasmodically; he was saving the place for Charlott!

I cannot let her go. Hating the knowledge, yet resigned to it, Brant levered himself up and reached for the phone on the bedside stand. Punching out Charlott's number on the tiny buttons on the inside of the receiver,

Brant gritted his teeth and muttered, "You'd better answer this time, damn you."

Except for the occasional gulping sob, Charley's spate of weeping had run its course. The crying binge had not brought the hoped-for release of tension or misery; in fact, she felt worse. Too spent to get up and hunt for a box of tissues, she sniffed repeatedly and wiped her cheeks with the back of her hand.

Why don't you go to bed, you silly woman? she asked herself scathingly. Go to bed and forget him and his cruelly sarcastic tongue that, when wielded in passion, could arouse the most incredible response in her.

Shivering with the delicious memory of her own unbridled desire, Charley leapt from the chair and ran into her bedroom, slamming the door as if by doing so she could bar the memory from following her. Of course she was unsuccessful.

Leaving her clothes where they dropped, Charley quickly undressed and slid a sheer cotton eyelet nightie over her head. Longing to escape the haunting recollection of gleaming black eyes and a slashing devil's smile, she grasped the bedcovers and pulled them back just as the phone on her bookcase headboard rang imperiously.

Stifling a groan, Charley stared at the instrument and berated herself for forgetting to turn on the answering machine. Biting her lip, she actually cringed as the phone continued to trill its summons. She knew who it was, but what did he want? Hadn't he already damaged her pride enough? Hesitating a moment longer, she listened to one more ring, then snatched the receiver from the cradle.

"He-hello?"

"Name it." Brant rasped in an angry snarl. "I will give you anything you want," he went on roughly, ignoring the gasp she emitted before clamping her lips together. "Anything, and everything, just name it, damn you. I'll expect your answer by Wednesday, at Dad's party. And you'd better show up, or I'll come looking for you."

Charley winced as his phone was slammed down.

How dare he damn me! Using fury to mask the pain clawing at her chest, Charley threw the receiver onto the cradle. Damn me, will he? Well, Mr. High Society Brant d'Acier, you are in for a rude awakening. Who needs you?

You do.

The taunting voice of her own conscience froze Charley in the act of getting into bed. Moving carefully, she slowly lowered her body onto the mattress. Her eyes shut tightly, she tried, and failed, to banish all thought of her tormenting caller. Fighting its way up from the depths of her subconscious, the tiny voice insisted on being heard.

You need him. You want him. Face it. Admit it. You love him.

"No!"

Charley sat bolt upright on the bed, completely unaware that she'd cried the denial aloud. No, she repeated silently, it is not possible to fall in love in less than forty-eight hours. I am fascinated by him. I am infatuated with him. I am sexually attracted to him. I am not . . . The thought trailed away, leaving Charley feeling raw.

How could you be so stupid? she demanded of herself. You, of all people? Haven't you suffered enough at the hands of this elite bunch of snobs? Will you now allow this half-breed son of a . . . scion of a once-titled family to trample your emotions?

Oh, Brant, she cried mutely. Why couldn't you be an unpretentious John Doe or the ordinary guy from next door? But she knew that if Brant had been different, she wouldn't have looked at him twice. Do you have a penchant for self-destruction? she asked herself wryly.

Wednesday. Three short days in which to come up with an answer that would put Brant off once and for all. What could she tell him? What demand could she make that Brant would be either unwilling or unable to meet? Though she scoured her mind, Charley continually drew a blank.

Positive she'd toss and turn all night, Charley actually drifted into a deep, restful sleep. She didn't wake until the summer sunlight opened her eyes the next morning.

Refreshed, Charley pushed the emotionally charged thoughts of the night before from her mind as she breakfasted on cold melon and hot coffee. There was work to be done. She would paint first, and think later, she decided as she strode to her studio to perform her morning ritual. She marched to the wall of windows to stare boldly out, then down, her fingers curling into her rapidly moistening palms.

Charley suffered from both acrophobia and vertigo. As she once told her friend Gayle, she could get lightheaded on a high curb. Though Charley could, and often did joke about her fears, there was nothing at all funny about them. Certainly there was nothing amusing about growing panicky at the sight of a window washer doing his job on a scaffold halfway up a towering building—and Charley did feel such panic. So, on each and every morning she forced herself to stand at her windows for long minutes, fighting the rising tide of nausea in an effort to cure herself of the malady; to date, Charley had been totally unsuccessful.

Smiling wryly in self-derision, as she also did each morning, she then turned to the love of her life—her work. Charley could no longer remember exactly when she'd lost her heart to drawing. All she knew was that she'd been quite young. Charley had never drawn "stick" people. Even at the age of six, if she drew a person, it looked like a person, usually someone she knew. At first her parents had been amused; her mother had claimed Charley had inherited the talent from Pegeen. By the time Charley was in her early teens her parents were chagrined, because they could not afford professional training for her, and it was obvious by then that Charley possessed a truly rare talent.

Strangely, or perhaps not so strangely, while Charley was in high school her teachers in art appreciation classes downgraded her artistic ability. Charley's work was undisciplined, they said. She was too flamboyant, too rash with her brush. At graduation she was bypassed and the college grants were awarded to those students who had consistently followed the precepts set down by their teachers. While lesser talents went on to higher education, Charley went to work in the lingerie department of one of the better department stores located in a shopping mall close to her suburban Philadelphia home. While working at the store Charley did not earn a lot of money, but she did acquire an appreciation for exquisite lingerie.

Six months after graduation, and two months after her mother succumbed to a congenital heart condition that had gone undetected all those years, Stephen Marks realized his first success. The irony was almost more than Charley could bear. Stephen, working long hours in his makeshift lab, unfunded and ignored, had developed a small, inexpensive machine that would enable physicians to detect just such potential heart problems during a routine examination.

Being brilliant but unsophisticated, Stephen sold the rights to his invention to a large company for what, at the time, seemed a considerable amount of money. In reality it was a paltry sum.

The following fall, at Stephen's insistence, Charley went off to a state college that boasted a superior art department. Before her sophomore year was over, Charley was both disillusioned and exalted at the same time. Her disillusionment was caused only partly by the discovery that her college instructors were just as rigid as those in high school.

An added disappointment was the attitude of her father's contemporaries. Even though Stephen had followed his first startling invention with several others of equal value, he was still not afforded the respect Charley knew was his due. Apparently ability and the beginnings of wealth—Stephen was growing more astute in financial matters—were not enough for high society.

But, by far the most disillusioning thing was the rejection Charley received from a young man, one of mainline Philadelphia's finest, after a brief romance and an even briefer engagement. Experiencing her first love at nineteen, Charley had been slavishly devoted to her handsome fiancé. On the night he'd given her a two-and-one-half-carat diamond engagement ring, Charley had come very close to surrendering her innocence to him.

Three days later, when the handsome young coward informed her of his parents' decision of her "unsuitability" as a bride, Charley thanked the moral scruples that had caused her to hold back.

Thus, disillusioned, disappointed, and disheartened at a most vulnerable time of her young life, Charley condemned what everyone else considered the cream of society. Deciding to play their game and beat them at it, she blithely ignored common sense when it chided her for indicting an entire segment of society for the cruelty of a few of its members. Deaf to the urging of her own intellect, Charley nurtured the hurt rather than let the scars heal. Afraid of love and its attendant commitment, she kept men at a distance by playing at flirtation. At twenty-five, incredible as she herself found it, Charley was still a virgin.

The exaltation she experienced during her sophomore year stemmed from the sale of one of her paintings to a publishing house for use as a book jacket. The money Charley earned from that and subsequent sales enabled her to study art in Paris.

During the years she spent in France, Charley perversely, deliberately, associated with the upper class, already laying the foundation for her reputation as a swinger with rather loose morals. Neither the crowd she cavorted with in Paris nor the friends she'd left back home were aware of the nature of her work. Leading a double life, scrupulously keeping her artistic successes a secret, Charley appeared to be a totally irresponsible, flamboyantly extravagant playgirl. Behind the dazzling smile she wore, Charley held society in contempt; Max Charles had no time to waste on the offspring of the rich and famous.

Now, on a brilliant summer morning, Charlott Marks perched on the edge of a high stool and studied the vivid, bold strokes she'd applied to a fresh canvas. The emerging scene of an arched suspension bridge was good, and Charley knew it. She always knew when a painting was really good, or merely adequate; the merely adequate never left her studio.

By working at a near fever pitch, Charley had not only covered a good deal of the canvas. She had managed to avoid thinking about Brant d'Acier. She decided to skip lunch so as not to break her concentration.

When Charley finally closed the studio door for the day, sunset was bathing the city in shimmering waves of gold. Drooping with weariness, she slid a frozen pot pie into the oven to bake while she attempted to wash away her tiredness under a steaming shower.

Revived by the shower, she dressed for the night in a jersey knit nightshirt and padded barefoot into the kitchen. She consumed her food hungrily while listening to the playback of her recorded telephone messages. There were many different voices on the tape, some male, some female. Noticeably absent was the deep timbre of the one voice she both longed and feared to hear.

Sighing in despair at her own conflicting emotions, Charley picked up the receiver and punched out the number of the only person whose call she intended to return.

"Hello?" Gayle Peters answered on the third ring. She sounded as tired as Charley felt.

"Hi, Gayle," Charley responded with false gaiety. "You rang?"

"Oh, Charley, yes!" Gayle exclaimed. "Where have you been all day?"

"Right here in my studio." Charley laughed tiredly. "Wearing out my brushes, so to speak."

"Not to mention yourself." Gayle sighed. "You do have a penchant for endeavors of Herculean proportions, don't you?"

"Good heavens! What big words you use, counselor," Charley replied, her laughter natural now. "Did you call for a reason, or did you just want to scold me?"

"For all the good that will do," Gayle chuckled. "I had a definite reason. I understand you're going to attend Louis d'Acier's party Wednesday evening?"

Charley's eyes widened in surprise. "Yes, but where did you hear that bit of information?"

"I ran into Luther Holtzman at lunch today," Gayle explained. "He told me you had agreed to go with him."

"I can't help but wonder how the subject came up," Charley mused aloud, annoyed yet unsurprised by Lou's indiscretion. He never could resist the opportunity to boast about concluding a successful deal or seeing a pretty woman.

"Well, actually, I brought up the subject," Gayle said softly, then added quickly, "You see, David asked me if I'd go with him, and I was trying to find out if any of the others of our crowd would be there."

Our crowd. Charley's lips curled at the clannish sound of Gayle's phrasing. In Charley's opinion, with the exception of Gayle and a few others, the members of "our crowd" were no more than a useless bunch of butterflies. One of the exceptions was David Beauchamps, an associate in the firm of lawyers where Gayle was employed. David had been trying to date Gayle for months, until now unsuccessfully.

Charley teased, "So, you've finally succumbed to David's blandishments?"

"Yes, but I'm afraid I have an ulterior motive." Gayle was nothing if not honest. "I . . ." she hesitated, then blurted out, "I'm fascinated with Louis d'Acier."

Brant's father? Charley frowned. Did Gayle mean what Charley thought she meant? But, then, what else could she mean? "Do you mean as in romantically fascinated?" Charley asked bluntly.

Gayle's voice was little more than a whisper. "Yes. I was introduced to him after you left the banquet Friday night and . . . and . . ." Her whisper trailed away to nothingness.

"Well, I'll be skinned!" Charley exclaimed. "I wonder if Mr. d'Acier owns a white charger?" She was referring to a long-standing joke between herself and Gayle. Though Gayle readily admitted that she hoped to marry someday, she rarely accepted invitations from the young men she came in contact with. Long ago Charley had teasingly accused Gayle of waiting for Prince Charming. Gayle responded to Charley's gentle taunt with a self-conscious laugh.

"You think I'm rather ridiculous, don't you?" Gayle murmured.

"Why would I think that?" Charley asked in confusion.

Now Gayle's laugh sounded embarrassed. "He *is* a bit older than I and, though he *was* charming, he's probably not the least bit interested in me."

A bit older! Charley's auburn eyebrows arched high.

Nearly thirty years separated Gayle and Louis; thirty years was a little more than a bit. Still, Charley was neither shocked nor worried for her friend. Hadn't she herself felt the man's charisma?

"Gayle," she said sternly. "Now I do think you're being ridiculous. If the man appeals to you, and he obviously does, what possible difference could the disparity in your ages make?" Charley had never judged people by age. She hastened to remind Gayle of that fact. "Counselor, I thought you knew my feelings on the subject of age."

"I did!" Gayle exclaimed, then, "I do . . . but, well, I guess I needed some encouragement."

"My dear friend," Charley spoke urgently. "If you believe in something, you should pursue it, regardless of what others might say or think."

"I often wonder exactly who is the counselor in our friendship," Gayle said with a soft chuckle. "Of course, that was exactly what I wanted to hear, and that was exactly why I called you. You never let me down. Thank you, Charley." She went on. "I'll see you Wednesday then?"

"Are you kidding?" Charley drawled. "I wouldn't miss this party for the world."

Chapter Seven

Brant d'Acier.

For the first time in three days Charley allowed herself to think of the man and the question he'd asked her Sunday night. It was late Wednesday afternoon and she was soaking in a tubful of jasmine-scented hot water. Thanks to her single-minded effort, the paintings were finished for her upcoming show and there was plenty of time for them to dry properly before being hung.

Tired but exhilarated, Charley lathered one long, silky leg. A shiver went through her at the idea of Brant stroking her bare skin.

Brant. A soft, longing sigh filled the quiet of the steamy white and gold tiled bathroom. What was she going to say to him tonight? Not for even one moment did Charley allow herself to hope that Brant would let her off the hook.

She had deliberately led him to believe she had a

price. Tonight Brant expected, no, demanded, that she state that price. Unfortunately Charley hadn't the vaguest idea of what to tell him. How did one go about placing a price tag on one's worth?

Still worrying, she completed her bath and stepped from the tub. Patting herself dry, Charley considered, then discarded her chances of employing delaying tactics. In her mind she could hear Brant's voice, roughly emphatic, as clearly as if he were standing beside her: *Name it. I will give you anything you want. Anything, and everything, just name it, damn you. I'll expect your answer on Wednesday, at Dad's party. And you'd better show up or I'll come looking for you.*

Staring into the wide blue eyes gazing at her in the cloudy mirror above the sink, Charley shuddered. She was preparing to go to Louis d'Acier's party, quaking at the thought of facing Brant.

After dressing in a shiny cotton pants ensemble that enhanced her height with its soft pale blue and mauve vertical stripes, Charley brushed her long, thick auburn mane into obedience. As she applied a light coat of makeup, she was no closer to finding an answer to Brant's question than she had been Sunday night.

You precipitated this charade, she told herself. You saw, you liked, you wanted, never imagining you'd finish by loving. Now what do you propose to do about it?

Dropping the sponge-tipped eye shadow applicator, Charley spun away from the bedroom mirror. I am not in love with him! she silently denied. I barely know the man!

You know, a tiny voice spoke from her subconscious. You know many things. You know the thrill of breathlessness caused by his smile. You know the tingle of expectation at the sound of your name on his lips. You know the excitement of watching his eyes darken with passion. You know the heat of arousal at the merest touch of his mouth. Oh, yes, you know many things, and all of them underline what you refuse to look at. Never have you felt quite this way about a man before. You, Charlott Marks, are in love, really in love, for the first time in your adult life—and the man wants to buy you!

Standing, head bent, in the middle of her expensively decorated bedroom, Charley listened to the gathering strength of her inner voice and admitted the truth of everything it told her.

Admittance was one thing; resolution was something else altogether! What *was* she going to say to him? Raking her mind, Charley slid her narrow feet into strappy slingback sandals of soft blue leather. She glanced at her reflection in the long mirror mounted on the closet door. The picture she made was one of casual, cool elegance—a distorted reflection if she ever saw one, she decided wryly as she left the room.

Luther was on time to the minute, which was hardly surprising. Luther was always on time to the minute! His appearance made a definite statement: young, good-looking, upwardly mobile, all-American. Luther was all of these and more. As a matrimonial catch, Lou was at the top of many an anxious mother's list. He was a success simply because he worked so very hard at it; not so much within the confines of his father's brokerage firm as in the drawing rooms and country clubs of the firm's clients.

Charley agreed that he was successful. Unfortunately she also considered him a crashing bore! She was bored with his flowery compliments, bored with his predictable little intimate dinner parties, and most bored of all with his attempts to talk her into bed. Charley was completely aware of why he was so persistent. Lou honestly believed that Charley had been to bed, at one time or another, with just about every one of his friends and, believing this, he felt left out; Luther Holtzman could not abide the thought of being left out of anything! Charley actually believed him when he insisted he was in love with her—insofar as she believed that *he* believed it!

Patiently enduring Lou's too soft, too moist kiss of greeting, Charley smothered a sigh and pulled away from him when his tongue timidly sought entrance to her mouth. A flashing, vivid memory of another male tongue, boldly thrusting past the barrier of her teeth, sent a shiver along her spine. Lou misinterpreted it as being caused by his own expertise.

"I know how you feel," he muttered thickly, skimming his wet lips over her cheek to her ear. "Oh, Charley! Why do you keep me hanging in suspense this way?" His moist breath sent a shudder of revulsion through her. "Why won't you say yes? It's not like I'd be invading sacred, untouched ground! Marry me, Charley. I know we'd make a brilliant match."

Right, Charley thought wryly, slipping out of his arms. Turning from him to pick up the slender clutch bag that matched her sandals, Charley allowed a tiny, bitter smile to play on her compressed lips. Silently she repeated his less than romantic proposal: *It's not like I'd be invading sacred, untouched ground!* Oh, right, indeed! We'd make some brilliant match! If Lou was unable to hook the sought-after client with his own inimitable charm, I could take over and clinch the deal in the bedroom!

Dismissing her thoughts with an unconcerned toss of her auburn hair, Charley turned back to Lou with a sugary smile. "Now, Luther," she purred. "We have plowed over this same ground so many times, I feel like I'm up to my knees in the furrow! I have told you, repeatedly, that I do not want to get married." Evading the arms Lou extended to embrace her once more, Charley circled around him and sauntered out of the apartment. "We had better leave." Tilting her head, she glanced back at him teasingly. "You wouldn't want to be late, would you?" Of course, her little ploy worked, but then, she had known it would!

His sky-blue eyes glowing with enthusiasm, Lou followed her along the hall to the elevator, his staccato sentences betraying his excitement over the contacts to be made at the party. Charley merely smiled tolerantly.

Brant spotted Charlott the minute she stepped onto the patio. For most of the last hour his narrow gaze had remained fixed on the long French doors that gave access to the terrace from the dining room. Raising the chunky glass he held in his right hand, Brant sipped at the Scotch and water he'd been nursing since his own arrival forty minutes before, and slid his glance slowly over her slender form.

In the obviously expensive pants outfit she was wearing, Charlott had the appearance of a haute couture model. As she glided across the flagstone patio, her elegant, loose-limbed gait reminded Brant of a sleek Thoroughbred racehorse.

The sport of kings. How apt, Brant thought, hiding a cynical smile behind his glass. Charlott—and the sport of kings. Though unflattering, Brant thought the analogy exceedingly apt.

Glittering with a combination of anger and desire, his dark eyes registered every detail about her, from the top of her red head to the tips of her mauve-tinted toenails. Every inch of her was beautiful, and Brant was determined to touch, taste, and possess every one of those inches.

I want to possess her! Since he had first seen her, incredibly less than one week ago, desire had solidified into rock-hard resolution. Brant was not a king, but he was a moderately rich man. Brant was also a realist, cognizant of the fact that everything had its price in one form or another. And, even if he had to mortgage his soul, Brant was prepared to meet Charlott's demands, whatever they might be. He had no choice.

Watching her with carefully concealed longing, Brant stiffened as a young man followed her onto the patio and slid his arm around her waist possessively. Brant bit back a vicious expletive. Luther Holtzman! What was Charlott doing with that on-the-make social climber? Brant swallowed the last of his drink as a familiar voice intruded softly into his thoughts of violence to the young stockbroker.

"That man who just walked out of the house. Do you know him, Brant?"

Shifting slightly, Brant gazed down at the small, lovely face turned up to him. "Yes," he answered in a controlled tone. "Why?"

The petite woman standing at his shoulder smiled shyly. "I . . . he's . . ." She paused, then murmured,

"He's very handsome." Her large dark eyes were entreating. "Would you introduce me to him, Brant?"

Brant's lips curved into a gentle smile. He felt a true liking for this lovely young Spanish-American woman who was his father's secretary . . . and who had been Brant's lover for a brief period of time. Brant's gentleness was a response to her nature; Nita Feyago had none of what is thought of as Latin temperament. She was sweet, and quiet, and always gentle.

"Ah, Nita," Brant teased. "When did you develop an interest in blonds?"

"The minute I saw him walk onto the patio," Nita replied candidly.

"You're serious!" Brant exclaimed, stunned that anybody, male or female, could be interested in the too handsome Luther Holtzman. Restraining the urge to laugh, Brant shrugged his shoulders. It seemed there really was no accounting for taste!

Nita bit her lip nervously. "Don't make fun of me, Brant, please."

"Ah, honey." Slipping his arm around her tiny waist, Brant turned to face her fully. "I'd never make fun of you." The only inkling he had that they were no longer alone was the spark of excitement that suddenly leaped into Nita's eyes. A softly drawling voice lit a corresponding spark of excitement in Brant's.

"I do hate to intrude on your intimate moment, Mr. d'Acier, but this gentleman would like to meet you. I can't imagine why."

Charley ignored Lou's murmur of censure as Brant slowly turned to pin her with his gleaming devil's eyes. Holding his stare steadily, she contrived to give him her most charming smile. What she ached to give him was a smack on his aristocratic mouth! Charley hated it; she deplored it; but she was insanely jealous. Damn him! How dare he proposition *her*, then smile beguilingly at another woman—a beautiful woman at that!

"This gentleman?" Brant's drawl mocked Charley's, and she gritted her teeth in fury. "You mean Luther?" Charley's eyes narrowed suspiciously.

Lou was not offended by Brant's veiled insult. Quite the contrary, he appeared delighted that Brant knew his name. Charley sighed for the hopelessness of the fool.

"I'm surprised, and pleased, that you know who I am, Mr. d'Acier." Lou actually gushed. "I've been wanting to meet you for some time now." Eagerly reaching out, he grasped the hand Brant had extended. "I've just had the pleasure of meeting your father," he rattled on. "I understand he has designed Charley's father's mansion."

"Yes, he has." Brant did not comment on the hows and whys of his knowing who Lou was. Instead, he indicated the woman standing beside him with a smile. "This young lady is my father's secretary, Nita Feyago. Nita, I'd like you to meet Stephen Marks's daughter, Charlott, and her . . . companion, Luther Holtzman."

The pause did not go undetected by Charlott. She fluttered her lashes at Brant, then turned to murmur polite niceties to Nita while measuring her up. The enthralled gaze the young woman was giving Lou brought a gurgle of laughter perilously close to Charley's lips. Unbelievable as Charley found it, Nita looked completely smitten with him.

Well, I will definitely be skinned . . . alive yet! Afraid she'd laugh out loud if she witnessed much more of the lovelight burning in Nita's dark eyes, Charley looked at Brant, fully expecting to see him glowering at the woman he had so recently smiled upon. The shock of finding Brant's eyes riveted on her own stole Charley's breath completely. Oh, Brant was angry, all right, but his anger was not directed at Nita or Lou who, amazingly, seemed fascinated by Nita. So much for Lou's undying love for me, Charley thought fleetingly, trying without success to tear her eyes from Brant's. Why was he so very angry at her? she wondered, raising her chin with bravado. And when would he take his eyes off her?

"Nita," Brant said, finally shifting his gaze to Nita and Lou, "I wonder if you'd mind entertaining Luther for a few minutes? Ms. Marks and I have a matter of . . . business to discuss."

Uncomfortably aware of the nature of Brant's "business," Charley stiffened imperceptibly, silently willing Lou to come to her rescue by objecting. Her mute plea went unheard by the fickle Lou.

"Take your time," Lou offered expansively, waving them off with a flicker of his soft-looking, manicured fingers.

"Of course I don't mind," Nita assured him, her eyes beginning to glow.

"It's really not necess—" Charley began, only to be rudely interrupted by Brant's harsh voice as he curled one hand around her upper arm.

"Come along, *Ms.* Marks, we'll go into Dad's study where we can discuss our *business* in private."

Without allowing her time to as much as sputter a protest, Brant strode off toward the house, forcing Charley to stretch her long legs in an effort to keep pace with him. She had formed numerous scathing indictments to fling at him once they were alone, but the instant she stepped inside his father's study, every one of them fled from her mind.

Frozen in place, Charley was deaf to the sound of the study door closing behind her. Her eyes wide with surprise, she stared at the painting on the wall. So this is where it's been all this time! Charley marveled, slowly walking across the room to stand staring up at it.

The painting of a modern-day madonna was one of Charley's favorites, and one of only a few whose whereabouts she had not known. When it had been shown almost three years ago, all Dani had told her was that it had been purchased by a client's representative. Now it was quite obvious the client had been Louis d'Acier!

"You like that, do you?" Brant's silky tone penetrated her preoccupation.

"Yes," Charley answered simply, honestly. "Do you?" Strangely she was suddenly eager for Brant's approval of her work. That shook her to the core; never had she sought anyone's approval!

"Yes. I like it very much." A small smile softened his set features. "Had I arrived at the gallery a few moments earlier on the day it was shown, I'd own it now. Dad beat me to this one."

This one? Charley was puzzling over his statement when he again drew her attention with a startling question.

"Would you like to own another Max Charles?" Before she could reply, Brant indicated the painting with a negligent movement of his hand. "Oh, not this particular work, Dad would never part with it. But, would you like some other piece by Charles?"

Beginning to see what Brant was getting at, Charley

arched her elegant brows disdainfully. "Is this your obscure way of inquiring if a painting by Max Charles is on my list of 'everything'?" she asked bluntly.

"Nothing obscure about it," Brant snapped. "Will a Charles do—for starters? I'm not so naive as to believe a Charles painting would be sufficient to secure your services indefinitely."

Her services! Her services! Charley was suddenly incensed. How *dare* he speak to her as if she were a high-priced call girl? Who did this . . . this upper-crust jerk think he was? Raising her hand, Charley almost slapped Brant across his arrogant face. The soft warning in his tone stayed her hand in midair.

"I wouldn't advise that, Charlott. I do not use physical abuse on a woman—except in retaliation." Walking slowly to her, he encircled her wrist with his long fingers. Drawing her hand to his mouth, he pressed the palm to his lips. He searched her face to catch the tiniest nuance of a reaction from her.

Charley's response to Brant's overt sensuality would have been hard to miss. A blatant shudder tore through her body, leaving her weak and feeling oddly shattered in its wake. Brant would have had to be hewn from solid granite not to both see and feel it. He proceeded to demonstrate to her that he was fashioned not of granite but of rock-hard muscle, and supple sinew, and warm, enticing flesh. Coiling his other arm around her waist, he eased her softness to the tautened length of his body.

"You see how it is with us, Red?" he murmured in an unsteady tone. "I have only to touch you to set the physical forces to work." He slid her palm across his smoothly shaven cheek, then lowered his head to brush her slightly parted lips with his own. "And the forces in

me are working overtime." His arm tightened spasmodically, flattening her against him, making her shockingly
aware of the exact meaning of his words.

All resistance and righteous indignation drained out of
her. Charley moaned deep in her throat and rose to her
toes to seek his teasing mouth with her own. Although he
drew his breath in sharply, Brant evaded her lips for an
agonizing second.

"If this was ever a game, played by either one of us, it
is over now, Charlott," he whispered roughly against
her trembling lips. "You told me you had terms. I told
you I'd meet them. I am fully aware you have a taste for
expensive things . . . rich things, and the time has come
for you to be explicit." Almost as if he could not stop
himself, Brant slowly slid his tongue along her bottom
lip. "I cannot, will not, wait much longer. I want you,
and I will have you." Before Charley's mesmerized
eyes, Brant's features hardened in determination. "Even
if it means putting myself into hock for the rest of my
life," he finished decisively.

Charley was given no time to respond in any way,
except with her lips. With Brant's kiss all the reasons
Charley had ever had for not becoming involved with a
man went completely out of her mind. She curled her
arms around his strong neck and clung to him, wanting
more of the delirium only Brant could give her. Deepening, deepening, the kiss went on and on until . . .

"Charley?" The sound of her name pierced Charley's
consciousness. "Are you in there?" The question drove
them apart. "Charley?" Gayle called again, rattling the
doorknob.

"Yes," Charley answered huskily, still gazing into
the dark depths of Brant's smoldering eyes. "Yes," she

repeated more strongly, stepping back, away from him. "Come on in, Gayle."

Brant cursed under his breath. Just as Gayle pushed the door open, he muttered, "You've bought yourself some time. I'll stop by your place after the party." He started to move away as Gayle entered the study and said for Charley's ears only, "And I'd better not find Mr. Blond Blah there either."

At the sight of Brant's imposingly large body striding toward her, Gayle hesitated two steps inside the room. "Oh, Mr. d'Acier! I didn't know you were in here! I'm sorry if I've interrupted something."

"You haven't," Brant assured her charmingly. He started through the doorway, then paused to glance back, a contemplative look on his face. "Gayle, is it?"

"Yes." Gayle smiled tentatively. "Gayle Peters. How do you do, Mr. d'Acier." A tiny frown wrinkled her brow at his odd expression, but Gayle extended a small hand.

"Quite well, actually." Brant's smile was breath-taking—at least it took Charley's breath. "Lawyer, aren't you?" he asked surprisingly, grasping her hand gently, briefly, inside his own.

Flustered, Gayle laughed nervously. "Yes, but how did you know about me?" She shot a glance at Charley; Charley shrugged her shoulders.

"Oh, I've been hearing quite a bit about you lately," Brant said, a smile twitching the corners of his lips. "All of it good, I assure you."

Gayle opened her mouth, but he forestalled her.

"Now, if you ladies will excuse me?" He raised a brow at Charley. "You won't forget our . . . appointment, will you?"

Charley gritted her teeth and smiled grimly. "No, I won't forget." And I won't be intimidated either! she added to herself.

As though he understood her silent warning, Brant laughed softly and strode out of the room, leaving the two women, one very angry and one very confused, to stare at each other. Charley was the first to blink away the overpowering effect of the man.

"You wanted to talk to me about something?" she asked Gayle.

"What?" Gayle murmured distractedly. Then, grinning, she asked, "Brant is a mite overwhelming, isn't he?"

I'll say! Charley kept the remark to herself, asking instead, "Whenever you're ready, counselor?"

Gayle blushed daintily. "Oh, yes! Charley! You have got to advise me about something!"

Containing a laugh at Gayle's excited chatter, Charley laid a calming hand on her arm. "Well," she mused aloud, "there's a switch. You're the one that gets paid to advise. Remember?"

"Char-ley." Gayle drew the name out on a wail. "This has nothing to do with legal matters. I need your advice on a personal matter."

"Ah, I see." Charley smiled conspiratorially. "It wouldn't have anything to do with Louis d'Acier, would it?"

Gayle frowned. "Yes, of course it would, but if you're going to tease me . . ."

"You *have* got it bad!" Charley exclaimed, cutting her off. "Okay, I won't tease you. Now, what's the problem?" she asked gently.

"Louis has asked me to stay after the party's over," Gayle told her morosely.

"I don't understand." Charley frowned. "Where's the problem in that? Don't you want to be alone with him? Get to know him better?"

"Certainly! But . . ." Gayle sighed. "Oh, I don't know, but I have this feeling, more from what he didn't say than from what he actually said, that he's going to tell me he thinks there's too big an age difference between us."

"And you're convinced the age difference means nothing?" Charley probed.

"Firmly convinced. He . . . he came to my apartment Monday night, not long after I talked to you on the phone . . ." Her voice trailed off, and there was a wisp of a smile on her lips.

"Go on," Charley urged, intrigued.

"We talked for a while, then just as he was leaving, he . . . he kissed me." Gayle moistened her lips in an unconscious, sensuous way, revealing her emotions before explaining them. "Charley, I have never been so"—she hesitated, as if groping for the exact term, then, shrugging, used the vernacular— "so turned on to a man in my life! You know, I've always been rather afraid of men."

Fascinated by this unguessed-at side of Gayle's personality, Charley nodded encouragingly. Gayle continued. "Well, at first, I mean when he began to kiss me, I simply froze, like I always had, then"—she swallowed —"then it was like I just caught on fire! I couldn't seem to get enough of him. And, to be perfectly frank, the last thing in the world I was thinking about was his age!

Good heavens!'' Now her cheeks went scarlet. ''I thought of a lot of things while his lips were on mine, most of them downright erotic! But I never once thought about the differences in our ages!'' Gayle drew a deep breath. ''I'll tell you, Charley, that man could very easily drive me crazy! You can't imagine!''

Oh, no? Charley had to fight the urge to laugh hysterically. Just goes to prove that the old adage is true: like father like son! Charley dragged her attention back to her friend.

''Charley, what am I to do?'' Gayle moaned.

Biting her lip, Charley stared at Gayle in indecision. Normally she neither gave nor asked for advice. But Gayle's obvious distress caused her to break her own rule.

''Tell him exactly how you feel,'' she suggested softly.

''Oh! But I couldn't!'' Gayle actually paled at the idea.

''Why not?'' Charley shrugged eloquently. ''We live in an age of enlightenment, in which women are allowed to be the aggressors. Besides, think of the position Louis is in. He must be feeling very insecure right now. You *are* nearly thirty years his junior.''

''But that doesn't mean a blasted thing to me,'' Gayle protested sharply.

''*I'm* convinced; now it's up to you to convince Louis!''

After the events of the first hour, the rest of the party should have been anticlimactic for Charley; it wasn't. There were too many charged undercurrents in the air. It started when she went for a swim in the kidney-shaped pool beyond the huge patio area. Charley had to dig her nails into her palms to keep from shivering when Brant's stare swept the length of her skimpily clad body.

Refreshed from her antics in the pool, which included a furiously paced game of water tag with some of the teenage guests, Charley made a round of the adult guests. More undercurrents. During her meandering she couldn't help noticing that Lou and Nita set off sexual sparks every time they looked at each other, which happened quite a lot.

Then there was the problem of her father. Stephen Marks had been a widower for eight years and Charley had begun to despair of his ever remarrying. Then, two years ago, Darlene Holt had entered their lives. Less than six months later it was apparent that she'd fallen in love—with her employer. Stephen, with his nose always buried in a book or in his lab, was completely unaware of how Darlene felt toward him.

Charley knew her father liked and admired Darlene. Charley also knew that her father possessed a strong sense of ethics. Never would he dream of stepping out of line with a woman in his employment. Charley's problem was how to wake him up without shaking him up!

Seeing Stephen drift alone over the extensive grounds surrounding Louis's home disturbed Charley almost as much as encountering Brant's blank stare every time she turned around.

While she moved through the line of hungry guests at the heavily laden buffet table, Charley's eyes danced with amusement as she observed Gayle undermining Louis's resolve by flirting with him outrageously. Romance seemed to be in the air.

Then, as she stood with her plate in one hand and a

glass of white wine in the other, glancing around for either Lou or for an empty table, Charley was startled by a soft whisper close to her ear.

"Wanna dance, kid?"

Smothering a shriek, and somehow managing to hang on to both plate and glass, Charley forced herself to turn slowly.

"You know, Brant," she snapped in exasperation, "although your lights are lit, I'm convinced there's nobody home in your second story! Will you go away and leave me to eat my dinner in peace—*please?*"

Brant, his hands also occupied with a plate and a glass, drawled, "If you don't want to dance, come have supper with me."

Groaning, Charley gazed up at him in defeat. "All right, Brant, I give up. You win . . . at least this round."

"About time too," he chided her. "You've won every one up till now."

It was not until they were settled at a table on the very fringes of the patio that Brant warned softly, "I always do win in the end, you know." His rakish grin did amazing things to Charley's heartbeat. "Chew that up with your supper."

Charley did consider his avowal as she devoured the delectable lobster bisque, cold steamed shrimp, and rice pilaf. Sipping her wine, she considered her chances of getting away with not being home to Brant later, after the party. What could he do to her really? she asked bravely. I shudder to think of what he is capable of doing to me! was the immediate answer.

Her dinner at least partially consumed, Charley finished her wine and rose from the table gracefully. She excused herself with a quickly fabricated lie. "I really must find a powder room. I—" Brant's soft laughter stopped the words in her mouth.

"Run away, wild one," he taunted softly. "The bell for the next round won't ring until after you're at home. And your lights had better be on," he gibed, throwing her earlier taunt back at her.

From the time she escaped Brant until the moment she ferreted out Lou in the romantic rose arbor where he was holding hands with Nita, Charley racked her brain for a delaying tactic to use against Brant. Unfortunately her usually agile mind drew a blank. She was in despair as she and Lou said their good nights until her glance settled on Gayle. And then inspiration struck.

"I'll be with you in a minute," she murmured to Lou and made her way to Gayle's side.

"Are you going to stay?" she asked, holding her breath.

"Only for a little while," Gayle sighed.

"Well, if you want to talk, and maybe come up with a better game plan," Charley said swiftly, urgently, "stop at my place on your way home. Together we should be able to think of something that will set Louis's fears at rest."

"Great." Gayle brightened. "It will be about an hour. Okay?"

Okay? An hour would be perfect! Charley was hard put not to laugh in sheer relief. Nodding in agreement, she hurried back to Lou.

During the drive to her apartment, Charley wisely remained silent and let Lou raise the subject of the dark-haired, dark-eyed Nita. Lou began slowly, fumbling around with apologies for deserting Charley for the majority of the evening. At Charley's solemnly given assurance that she was not at all insulted or even mildly upset, Lou practically gushed about the young woman.

When at last Lou stopped the car and his endless rhapsodizing, Charley was more certain than ever that he was an utterly boring man!

A devilish thought slipped into her mind as she waved good night to him. Chuckling softly, she thought, Brant was right, Lou *is* Mr. Blond Blah!

Chapter Eight

It was exactly eleven thirty-seven when Charley closed the door to her apartment. It was exactly eleven forty-three when she opened it again to admit Brant.

"What kept you?" she asked bitingly, turning her back on him and sauntering to the couch.

"I was held up in traffic," Brant replied smoothly, following her. Dropping onto the far end of the couch, he stretched his long legs out, crossed his ankles, and smiled teasingly. "Otherwise I'd have been here sooner."

Charley yawned openly. "Too bad. You missed the big love scene," she lied sweetly. "Lou was excitingly reluctant to let me go."

Never had Charley seen anybody move with such swiftness and agility. Almost before the last taunting word passed her lips, Brant had slid down the length of the couch. His face, frightening in its harshness, loomed over hers.

"If he touched you, I'll break every bone in his body," he snarled. "Very slowly, one by one."

"You'll do nothing of the kind! You have no right threatening my . . . ah . . . gentlemen friends." Charley knew immediately that her phrasing had been unwise. Even though she would not have believed it possible, Brant's features tightened even more with anger.

"I have the right of highest bidder," he informed her nastily. "What did *he* offer you?" They were nose-to-nose now. "Dead animal skins? Stones somebody went grubbing in the ground for?" A sneer twisted his beautifully shaped lips. "A pile of motorized metal with an enormous price tag?"

Feeling tired, harried, and altogether at the end of her tether, Charley glared directly into his glittering black eyes. How she longed for a stinging retort that would put an end to this farce once and for all. And then, as so often happens, inspiration unexpectedly dawned. Why haven't I thought of it before? Charley wondered.

"I'll tell you what Lou offered me," she retaliated softly. "He offered protection, respectability, legality."

Holding her breath, Charley watched as Brant's eyelids narrowed in speculation. When Brant spoke it was through teeth tightly clamped together. "He asked you to marry him?" he ground out disbelievingly.

"Exactly," Charley said smugly.

"And your answer was what?" Brant snapped.

Although Charley had been expecting the question, she hesitated before responding to it. She could lie, or tell Brant the truth. If she lied to him, he'd realize it before too long but, if she told him the truth, she'd be right back at square one, with Brant nagging at her to attach a price tag to herself.

Charley sighed with relief when she was literally saved by the bell—her own doorbell. Thanks to her forethought, this time it was Gayle to the rescue!

"I absolutely do not believe this!" Brant's exclamation was punctuated by another trill of the bell. "Don't tell me; let me guess," he groaned. "Your father, right?"

"No." Charley tried not to laugh. Brant looked so frustrated! Served him right for forcing himself on her! "I believe it's Gayle." That was the truth; Charley could only *believe* it was Gayle until she opened the door. "She has a problem she needs to discuss with me." That also was the truth, as far as it went; who said she had to confess to inviting Gayle to stop by after the party?

"Gayle has a problem?" Brant closed his eyes as if in pain. "And she had to discuss this problem at midnight?" he gritted out, wincing when the bell pealed once more.

"Midnight or ten in the morning." Charley shrugged, slipping by him to hurry to the door. "What difference does it make?"

"To me?" Brant grated, stalking her footsteps. "One hell of a lot of difference." As Charley reached for the lock he leaned closer to her ear. "I suppose you're going to tell her I was just leaving?"

In truth, that was exactly what Charley had planned on saying, but an idea struck her even as she opened her mouth to concur. "Nooo," she purred choosing her words carefully. "I think it would be better if you hung around awhile." With a twist of her fingers she released the lock, giving him no time to reply. "You may be better able to advise her than I."

With that, Charley swung open the door to reveal an anxious-looking Gayle. When she saw Brant her expression changed from anxiety to chagrin. Instead of entering, Gayle stepped back into the hall.

"Oh, Charley, I—I'm sorry! I didn't realize! I mean . . ."

Stepping into the hall, Charley grasped Gayle's arm and drew her into the apartment. "Of course you didn't realize," she agreed soothingly. "How could you? But it doesn't matter." Then, as Gayle resisted the tug of Charley's hand, she coaxed, "We can still talk. Brant has offered to leave." Brant made an exasperated sound. "But, I've asked him to stay."

Gayle began to back up again. "Uh, yes, well, I think I'd rath—"

"Gayle, really!" Grabbing her friend, Charley pulled her into the room and quickly closed the door. "Will you think, counselor? Who knows Louis better than Brant?"

"Louis?" Brant repeated softly. "As in Louis d'Acier?"

Charley's sigh was long-suffering. "Of course, Louis d'Acier," she answered, somehow managing to herd him and Gayle into the kitchen. "I'm going to have some coffee. Will that do for you two, or would either one of you prefer something else?"

"Coffee's fine," Gayle murmured, eyeing Brant warily.

"Suits me," Brant muttered, eyeing Gayle speculatively.

Silence reigned while Charley deftly prepared the coffee. It was Charley herself who initiated the discussion after they went back into the living room with their mugs.

"Okay," she sighed, glancing from Gayle to Brant, then back at Gayle. "Somebody has got to start the conversational ball rolling, or we'll be here all night." Ignoring the pleading look Gayle threw at her, Charley looked Brant directly in the eye and said bluntly, "Gayle is . . . ah . . . interested in your father—very interested."

Brant, like Charley, chose to ignore Gayle's murmur of protest. Returning Charley's straightforward stare, he queried softly, "Romantically interested?" At Charley's nod, he went on, obviously puzzled. "So, what's the problem?"

They both ignored Gayle's attempt to be heard. "Your father, although he admits to a reciprocal interest, maintains that he is too old for Gayle," Charley told him.

"Ah, yes," Brant breathed. "Dad would. He's a real gentleman, you know."

"Yes, I know he is," she responded. "Now, the problem is, how does Gayle go about changing your father's mind?"

Brant shot a glance at Gayle. "Are you serious about my father, or are you indulging in some sort of older-man fantasy here?"

Oh, boy! Charley groaned inaudibly, almost afraid to look at Gayle. Expecting her friend to either cringe at Brant's direct probe or bristle angrily, she was amazed at Gayle's calm response.

"I suppose there is an element of fantasy involved, Brant. But, please believe that I'm not playing games."

"I appreciate your honesty, Gayle, but I'm afraid it

doesn't go quite far enough. Exactly what does this fantasy entail?''

Gayle hesitated long enough to draw a deep breath, then plunged into an explanation of her motives. "I'm thirty years old and not only unmarried but more often than not undated.''

"Only by choice!" Charley inserted loyally.

Gayle smiled softly. "Thank you, Charley.'' Returning her gaze to Brant, she elaborated. "You see, Brant, by and large men frighten me.'' Gayle's shoulders rose in a small shrug. "I don't know why, exactly. I can trust them in a business situation but, when it comes to a personal relationship, I get nervous. Even though we haven't known each other long, I trust your father implicitly. I don't know, maybe I have a father-figure complex or something. What I do know is I have never felt about any man the way I feel about Louis. I realize he's thirty years older than me, but my feelings are so strong that I'm convinced that even if we have only five years to share, they would be the best and happiest five years of my life.'' Glancing away, Gayle swallowed with obvious difficulty then, bringing her eyes back to Brant's, she smiled. "The defense rests.''

Several minutes passed in total silence and Charley was on the verge of jumping up to hug Gayle when Brant said quietly, "That was some impassioned plea you made for your client, counselor. You have swayed this jury of one.'' Drawing his chair closer to the coffee table in a no-nonsense way, he motioned Charley to refill their cups. "Now, how can I help you convince him that you're the best thing to happen to him since sliced bread?''

They talked for over an hour then, and Brant finally

decided that their best chance of undermining Louis's resolve was bombardment from the outside—from Gayle —and sabotage from the inside—via Brant. Without a hint of hesitation Brant promised, ''I'll sing your praises, Gayle, and lay on the compliments with a trowel.''

When finally Charley closed the door behind Gayle and Brant, who left together, she was smiling. Gayle's campaign of the heart was well under way, and Charley had successfully avoided a romantic confrontation with Brant.

Long after Gayle and Brant had said good night, Charley lay upon her bed thinking of her own problem. She had to decide what to tell Brant about her answer to Lou's proposal. If she told him the truth, admitting she'd turned Lou down flat, she was positive Brant would increase his efforts to seduce her. On the other hand, if she lied, telling him she'd agreed to marry Lou, it would not be very long before Brant got wise to the situation. Either way Charley lost and Brant won!

Charley finally fell asleep somewhere around dawn, only to dream she was being chased by a satyr who was wearing an Indian headdress fashioned from the head of a wolf.

After dragging her weary body off the bed late Thursday morning and making a quick stop in the kitchen for hot coffee, Charley performed her daily ritual. She walked to the studio windows to look out and down, but she did not linger in her workroom as usual. Instead, she turned away, palms damp, stomach queasy, and walked out again, firmly closing the door behind herself. After the endless weeks of work she had put in completing the canvases for her upcoming show, Charley decided she'd earned a vacation—and then some!

With a second cup of coffee in hand, Charley stood at the stove waiting for an egg to poach and asked herself what she could do to outrage society and amuse herself.

Some twenty minutes later she ate the last mouthful of her breakfast and refilled her cup for the third time, wondering why none of the wild ideas she'd come up with appealed to her. Maybe I'm becoming jaded, she mused, putting her dishes into the dishwasher.

Or maybe you are finally growing up, her conscience suggested. Ridiculous! Striding out of the kitchen, Charley dismissed the thought.

More than ridiculous, the tiny voice in her mind agreed. All these years of one ridiculous caper on top of another. What *was* the point of displaying your body in old dowager VanZant's pool? Where was the advantage in being escorted to banker Tarrelton's dinner party by a sinister-looking member of the underworld? What was the purpose of driving ninety miles an hour in your overpriced sports car?

All right! Charley silently screamed at the nagging voice, I behaved like a nit! She suddenly realized that she'd been pacing back and forth in front of the table that held the phone. If she was honest with herself, she had to admit she'd been expecting, no, hoping, that it would ring. And she had to admit she longed to hear only one voice on the line.

Damn it! Mumbling to herself, she stormed into her bedroom to dress. All she had wanted to do was to have a little fun with Brant.

At his expense, her conscience prompted.

Scowling at her own reflection in the mirror, Charley

slipped into white designer jeans, a thin cotton camisole top, and high-heeled shoes. After wielding a brush punishingly on her hair, she tossed it back away from her face, scooped up her shoulder bag, and tore out of the apartment, refusing to recognize her hasty departure as flight.

Driving under the speed limit for the first time in years, Charley turned the bright orange sports car in the direction of her father's house. The car didn't even drive smoothly, she realized, also for the first time. Why had she ever bought the thing? she wondered irritably. She wasn't even fond of the color orange!

Becoming more ashamed and embarrassed by the outrageously juvenile behavior she'd been indulging in, Charley sighed with relief as she turned the car onto the drive leading to the old, narrow house her father had bought seven years before. She had expected to find her father working in his lab, so she was pleasantly surprised to find him puttering around in the flower beds that flanked the drive at the rear of the house.

"Hi, skinny," Stephen called as she slid out from under the steering wheel. "Are you escaping from your easel?"

"No." Not the easel, she added silently, but a dark-eyed devil. "I finished up the work yesterday." She bent to kiss his cheek. "I decided to take a break before starting my next masterpiece."

"You look different somehow," Stephen remarked, noting the absence of makeup and the serious expression on her face. "Are you feeling all right, honey?" he asked.

"Actually, no," Charley answered honestly, surprising herself.

"Do you want to talk about it?" Stephen asked, concerned. Charley hadn't admitted to anything but being on top of the world since she'd celebrated her eighteenth birthday.

"No." Charley took an agitated step away, then turned back. "Yes! If . . . you want to listen?"

Stephen sprang from his kneeling position with the agility of a man twenty years younger than he. Brushing the dirt from his hands and knees, he strode toward the house, suggesting, "Let's go into my study—after I've washed my hands."

Entering the kitchen by the screen door, Stephen made a straight line for the downstairs bathroom. Charley waited for him in the kitchen, passing the time in conversation with Darlene. During the two years that Darlene had worked as housekeeper for Stephen, she and Charley had become close friends. Darlene was one of the select few who knew of Charley's pseudonym.

"How is the work for the show shaping up?" Darlene asked interestedly, her examination of Charley's face every bit as shrewd as Stephen's had been.

"All done," Charley replied negligently, fully aware she wasn't fooling Darlene for a moment. "I'm taking a short vacation from my studio."

"About time," Darlene snorted. Darlene was also one of the few people who knew Charley worked much harder than she played. "You work too hard." Looking down at Charley from her superior height, the older woman said bluntly, "You ought to get married and stop all this funny business you've been wasting your time on."

Merely hearing the word *married* tightened Charley's already taut nerves, and she snapped, "Look who's talking! Why don't *you* do something to open my father's eyes, then drag *him* down the aisle?''

It was hard to determine who was more shocked by the outburst, Darlene or Charley herself. Recovering, Darlene was on the point of rebuttal when Stephen returned to the kitchen, ending what promised to be an argument. Rummaging in the fridge, he grabbed two tall bottles of cola, then strode out again, calling, ''Coming, skinny?''

''Coming,'' Charley called back, pausing only long enough to whisper, ''I'm sorry, Darlene. I ought to have an operation to have the barbs removed from my tongue. Please try to forget what I said.''

''Who's the man, Charlott?'' Darlene responded.

Charley was at once flustered and defensive. ''What man? There is no—''

''Don't even try to con me, Charlott Marks.'' With a wave of her hand she indicated the doorway to the hall. ''Your father is waiting. You can come back and lie your head off after your business with him is concluded.''

Duly chastised, Charley meekly left the room to join Stephen in his study. She was beginning to think she'd made a mistake in agreeing to talk with him. If Darlene could see through her so easily, her father would have no trouble getting to the heart of the matter.

Sure enough, Stephen came right to the point. ''Brant pressuring you, is he?'' he demanded in an ominously quiet tone.

Heaving a sigh, Charley walked to the narrow window and stood staring out at the side yard. ''I'm afraid I've been very foolish, Dad.''

''In what way have you been foolish?''

His abrupt question drew her around to face him and

Charley was startled by the fierceness of his expression. There was more here than met the eye. As if a recording had suddenly been turned on, Charley heard Stephen and Brant's conversation of the previous Friday night. "You don't waste any time. Do you?" her father had asked Brant. And then Brant had replied, "There has been no pressure applied here." What had gone on between the two men earlier that evening at the party? Surely Brant hadn't had the arrogance to inform her father of his plan to buy his way into her bed? Oh, no? she chided herself, knowing, by now, that Brant had very likely told her father of his plans bluntly and succinctly. No wonder her father had been so concerned about her that night. Today, too, come to that!

"Charlott!" Stephen's tone snapped her out of her reverie. "I asked you in what way have you been foolish?"

For one moment longer Charley hesitated, then she blurted out, "I'm very much afraid I've fallen in love with Brant, Dad." Charley caught her lower lip between her teeth and gnawed at it while she waited for his reaction. When it came, it was with a sigh and not the roar she'd expected.

"Is there any chance Brant feels the same way about you?"

"He"—Charley swallowed—"he wants me," she whispered.

"That's not what I asked you," Stephen observed.

Charley drew a deep breath. "I know." Turning away, she strode back to the window, then spun to face him again. "I'm as much, if not more to blame than Brant is, Dad. I allowed him, *led* him and everyone else, to believe that I . . . that I—"

"I know," Stephen cut in sadly. "Oh, honey, I was so very afraid that something like this would happen and you'd be hurt." Getting to his feet as though he was suddenly very tired, Stephen walked to her and enfolded her protectively in his arms. "You've been so bitter and headstrong." Smoothing his hand over her glorious hair, he sighed. "A bad combination. Somebody was sure to get injured. I was always afraid it would be you."

"And rightly so." Forcing a weak laugh, Charley leaned back to gaze into his beloved face. "And I can never claim you didn't try to warn me. You did— repeatedly. But I was positive I'd continue to laugh at the havoc I created." She shook her head. "Suddenly I simply don't feel like laughing." Burrowing her face in his chest, she wailed, "Oh, Daddy, what am I going to do? You see, I want Brant as much as he wants me."

"You could tell him," Stephen ventured softly. "I mean everything." Before Charley could even gasp in shock, he asked, "Does he know about your work?"

"No." She straightened up. "You know, it's almost funny. Brant greatly admires the paintings of Max Charles." Her laughter had the sound of a sob. "He even offered to buy me one as an inducement! Isn't that a scream?" She moved away from her father, distractedly rubbing her palms along her jean-clad thighs. Then with a jerky movement she whipped around to face him again. "Oh, by the way, my modern madonna is hanging in Louis's study!"

"I know." Stephen smiled. "I saw it there last night. Louis is very admiring of you, you know." At her startled look, he hastily added, "Louis admires Charlott Marks. He is unaware that you are Max Charles."

"I can't imagine why," Charley drawled. "I am something of a . . ."

"Charlott," Stephen warned softly. "Be careful how you malign the daughter I adore." Then, briskly, he made up his mind. "I think you should confess all to the young savage. A good setdown would serve that arrogant whelp right!"

"I don't know, Dad." In truth Charley felt she didn't quite have the courage to confront Brant with her own duplicity. "I'll . . . think about it. Maybe. Someday. Right now, I just want to fade into the sunset."

"Would you like *me* to talk to him?" Stephen offered gently.

"Good heavens, no!"

Stephen appeared disappointed. "Well, if you should change your mind, let me know." A grin split his face. "I would love twisting that young lion's tail."

Charley was both appalled and amused at the same time. "Don't you like Brant, Dad?"

"Not like Brant?" Stephen laughed. "Of course I like him! And, at least professionally, I respect him. I'd say he's just a mite too arrogant and self-confident if I hadn't suffered from the very same condition myself all these years." His laughter dwindled to a chuckle. "As a matter of fact, until last Friday I thought he was the best thing to come down the pike since Superman!" His laughter died completely and his features set into a mask of anger. "But I will be damned if I'll stand by and watch him hurt my little girl!"

"I'm hardly a little girl anymore, Dad." A sad, wistful smile softened her lips. "By twenty-five a girl should have her head together enough to avoid being hurt."

"Even so . . ." Stephen began roughly. Charley silenced him with a sharp shake of her head.

"I walked right into this, Dad. Now all I have to do is figure out how to walk away from it."

"If he'll let you," Stephen said bluntly.

"Yes, *if* he'll let me," Charley echoed solemnly, turning slowly to gaze sightlessly through the window.

A silence settled on the room. In the uneasy quiet Stephen's sigh had the effect of a gunshot.

"Men are not very wise when they want something badly, and even less so when that something is a woman."

Charley went still, listening to the echo of her father's harsh tone. She was suddenly very certain Stephen was saying a lot more than he had actually said! Could it be that he was referring to his situation with Darlene as well as Brant's with Charley?

Casually Charley turned to examine her father's face, searching for the tiniest nuance that would betray his unspoken meaning. Unaware of Charley's perusal, Stephen let his face reveal his emotions.

Incredible! It would appear, she mused, that living over a half century was no guarantee of maturity when it came to the age-old question of attraction between the sexes! Unless she was reading the signs wrong, and Charley felt sure she was not, her father was pining for a woman. Deciding at that instant that she had to know the truth, Charley determined to find out if Darlene was the woman.

"Speaking of liking people, Dad," Charley began carefully, "don't you particularly like Darlene?"

The effect of her query was immediate and satisfying. Stephen visibly stiffened, his head jerked up, jaw thrust forward. "What do you mean?" he growled. "Darlene is a wonderful woman, and you know it, Charlott!"

"Oh, yes," Charley agreed, hiding the smile that teased her lips. "I know it. I was merely curious to know whether or not *you* knew it."

"You're up to something." Stephen's eyelids narrowed. "Spit it out, skinny. What's on your mind?"

"You," Charley answered serenely. "And Darlene. And the fact that the both of you work so very hard at hiding your feelings from each other."

Stephen's fierce frown probably would have put any other person off. But Charley saw through his frown to the glimmer of hope awakening in his eyes. His question confirmed her suspicions.

"Exactly what do you mean by *both* hiding feelings?"

"Oh, Dad, really!" Charley feigned exasperation. "Anyone can see that Darlene practically worships the ground you walk on." She shook her head in despair. "Even you must have realized that she's been spoiling you rotten since she started working here! Good Lord! The woman waits on you like a personal slave!"

"Yes, she does, doesn't she?" Stephen's expression might have been comical if it hadn't been so heartwarmingly endearing. "Do you really think Darlene . . . ah . . . cares for me in that way?"

Charley smiled teasingly at her obtuse father. "I don't think *cares* quite defines what Darlene feels for you," she said gently. "The question is—how strong are your feelings for her?"

"After nearly two years?" Stephen exclaimed revealingly. "I'm about ready to climb the walls!" To Charley's surprise and delight a dark flush stained his cheeks.

After clearing his throat self-consciously, Stephen went on in obvious embarrassment. "I suppose you think it's pretty funny. I mean, a fifty-two-year-old man itching like a teenager to get his hands on a woman?"

Moving quickly, Charley went to him where he stood, in the middle of the room, looking shocked at his own admission. Circling his still trim waist with her arms, she hugged him fiercely, murmuring, "No, Dad, I do not think it's funny." Rubbing her face against the soft material of his shirt, she scolded, "I think it's sad that you've wasted so much time."

"Then . . ." He hesitated, wetting his lips nervously. "Then you really feel I should approach Darlene about it?"

"Nooo," Charley crooned. "I really feel you should tell her flat out exactly how you feel. And I think you should do it at once, before you have time to chicken out and change your mind." Laughing up at him, Charley released her hold on him and stepped back. "I'm going now."

"Charlott!" Stephen's voice held a touch of fear. "Wait!"

"Nope." Charley's long strides had already carried her to the door. "I'm clearing the field of outside influences." She managed to look stern. "Don't disappoint me now, Dad. But, more importantly, don't disappoint Darlene." Charley walked out of the room, then poked her head back in. A bright smile lit her entire face as she added, "I fully expect to receive the good news from either you or Darlene before the week is out, and as there are only two days left to this week, you'd better get moving."

Charley was still chuckling at the terrified expression on her father's face when she strode into the kitchen on her way out.

"You're not leaving already?" Darlene protested seeing Charley head for the back door.

"You bet." Charley couldn't help it, her chuckle just naturally grew into a laugh. "I'm not hanging around here only to find myself a third wheel."

Darlene's frown conveyed her confusion. "I don't understand."

"You will," Charley promised, pushing open the screen door. "Oh, yes, indeedy, you certainly will." Not giving the older woman time to respond, Charley called, "I'll very likely be talking to you soon. 'Bye!"

Charley was almost halfway home when her thoughts went to the original reason for her visit to her father: Brant d'Acier. Had he attempted to reach her? Charley bit her lip. Or, more upsetting still, had he decided to forget her? It was at that point that she realized she had forgotten to switch on her answering machine.

She was calling herself forty-five kinds of a nincompoop by the time she arrived at her apartment. But as she turned the key in the lock she heard the beautiful sound of her telephone ringing. Her elation evaporated as soon as she snatched up the receiver and identified her caller.

"Oh, hello, Lou," she responded dully to his bright greeting. "What's on your mind on this disgustingly gorgeous afternoon?"

"What's wrong, Charley? Hung over—again?"

Lou's easy laughter went through her like a wailing siren at midnight. His observation, which once would have been exactly the one she'd been working so hard to achieve, annoyed her now. Charley had never been hung over in her life, but she had used the excuse to gain privacy more times than she cared to remember.

"Yes," she snapped. "So make it quick." Somebody else might be trying to call me at this very moment! she added mutely. "What do you want, Lou?"

"Well . . . uh . . . I . . ." Lou's urbane manner appeared to desert him suddenly. "Charley," he said. "About my proposal last night?"

"Yes?" Feeling mean, Charley reminded him, "And last week. And the week before that. And the week before that . . ." She deliberately let her voice trail away before asking, "What about it?"

"Ah, you did say no," Lou blurted out. "Didn't you?"

"Did I?" she cooed.

"You know you did!" Lou yelped. "Charley, you won't hold me to it?" he pleaded.

"No, Lou." She let him off the hook gently. "I won't hold you to it." Even though she really couldn't have cared less, she asked, "You really fell for Nita, didn't you?"

"Yes," Lou replied hoarsely. "I know it sounds crazy, but I think I fell in love at first sight! Can you believe it?"

Can I believe falling in love at first sight? The question revolved in Charley's weary mind long after she'd said good-bye to Lou. And the answer was always an emphatic yes.

Charley paced the floor in front of the phone throughout the rest of the afternoon and into the early evening, forgetting everything, even the necessity for food. When the phone finally did ring at precisely seven past eight, Charley was so keyed up, she practically growled into the receiver.

"Have you been drinking?" Brant demanded sharply.

At the end of her rope, Charley snarled, "What's it to you, buster?"

"I'll tell you what it is to me, *honey*," Brant snarled back, leaving no doubt whatever that his term was decidedly not an endearment. "I don't want my woman turning into a lush."

"Your woman!" Charley shouted. *"Your* woman? Live in hope, die in despair, *chum*." Even loving him, Charley was not going to tolerate his arrogance. "If you will remember, Mr. d'Acier, another man has first dibs."

"What can that jerk give you!" Brant shouted back at her.

"Let me explain the facts of life to you, Brant," Charley said sweetly, gritting her teeth. "Unbelievable as it may seem, the most important thing on this earth to many, many women, is still marriage. Got that, *friend?*" With that, she slammed the receiver down with a satisfying bang.

Chapter Nine

Everything. The earth, and all the best things on it.

Marriage.

Damn!

The sound of the phone slamming down on the other end of the line was still ringing in Brant's ears as he replaced his own receiver.

She is going to marry Luther Holtzman! Well, good riddance, Brant thought savagely. Holtzman is welcome to her! They deserve each other; make the perfect couple. A mealy-mouthed social climber and a twenty-five-year-old enfant terrible, spoiled by too much freedom, too much attention, too many men!

They deserve each other! Closing his eyes, Brant fought against the image of Charlott, naked upon a bed, her satiny skin shimmering in the glow of soft lighting, her lucious lips parted, her slender arms upraised in invitation . . .

An uncomfortable clenching sensation surrounded his chest and Brant winced at the feeling of having all the oxygen ruthlessly squeezed from his body.

Damn it! She is mine!

Breathing raggedly, Brant forced his long fingers to release their death grip on the chair arms. Don't be a fool! the faint voice of reason cautioned. You know her less than a week, and what you do know *of* her does not bear thinking about! Let Lou have her. He's probably had her already! He, and every other man in this city who has her price in his bank account!

But she is mine!

Sighing in both defeat and relief, Brant snatched up the telephone again.

Charley sat curled into the corner of her expensive couch chewing her lower lip and fighting to contain the flow of tears. It's for the best, she told herself bracingly. Good heavens, you barely know the man! Consider yourself well rid of him. In the end you would have been hurt . . . much more than you are now.

A tear rolled down her cheek. Was it possible to hurt more than she was hurting now? Charley moved her head from side to side. The pain would lessen, then disappear . . . someday . . . if she lived long enough.

Startled by her own train of thought, Charley brushed her hand over her wet cheeks. I can't be in love with him; I simply cannot! He is virtually a stranger! Who is Brant d'Acier anyway? Just another handsome face, an arrogant, overconfident member of the top-drawer crowd! One of the despicable ones.

But I do love him!

The tears streamed down her face. At that moment the

phone had the temerity to ring. Sniffing inelegantly, Charley glared at the slim white instrument, advising herself not to answer its summons. The ring went on and on until, afraid she'd go mad from listening to it, she snatched up the receiver. "Hello?"

"Okay, Charlott, you win."

Charley gasped at the sound of Brant's hoarse voice, and blinked in confusion at his words. What was Brant playing at now? Suddenly wary, Charley drew a deep breath before trusting herself to reply.

"What are you talking about, Brant?" she asked with what she thought was commendable coolness.

"Protection, respectability, legality," Brant threw her own words of the night before back at her. "You want marriage . . . I'll give you marriage."

Oh, dear God! He was still trying to buy her! Though it was the hardest thing she'd ever had to do in her life, Charley sealed her lips against the eager "yes" that sprang to her tongue. Desperate now, she used anger to ward him off.

"What a charming proposal! Your eloquence betrays your French heritage, or is it your savage blood asserting itself?"

"Can the sarcasm," Brant warned, sounding very near the end of his patience. "Are you going to marry me or not?"

"Why should I?" she shot back.

"Because I can give you more, one helluva lot more, than Lou Holtzman ever can," he said nastily. "And you can attach any meaning you like to that promise."

Charley's gasp was audible. Disgusted with Brant and with her own insidious excitement at his words, Charley replied, "I'll let you know, later, if you're lucky."

Without an ounce of regret Charley hung up on him again.

The regret came later—about thirty seconds later. Charley switched on the answering machine and fled to her studio. She worked furiously, stroking vivid oils onto canvas in an attempt to block out the recriminating thoughts that hammered for attention inside her head. Hours later, when she moved stiffly away from the easel, she stepped back to get a long view of the seascape she'd created with paint. The painting was of an angry sea flinging itself against a gray rock-strewn beach. Above, the sky was laden with black clouds rent by jagged streaks of lightning.

Charley turned her back on the painting and walked from the room, closing the door behind her with finality. She, too, felt stormy and restless as a churned-up sea.

Reduced to exhaustion, Charley swallowed a glassful of orange juice for supper, stood under a stingingly hot shower, then fell into bed to escape into unconsciousness for twelve solid hours.

She woke hungry, rested, and miserable. Contemplating her complicated situation over a bowl of cold cereal and a cup of hot coffee, Charley came up with what she thought was an absolutely brilliant plan.

Carrying her second cup of coffee into the living room, she settled down on the couch, disconnected the answering machine, and punched out the number of the Dani Longlott Art Gallery.

"Longlott Gallery," Dani answered brightly on the third ring.

"Hi, Dani." Charley greeted her friend, then dove right to the heart of the matter. "Is it too late to add some info to the publicity for the showing?"

"No," Dani answered. "At least I don't think so. Why, what did you want to add?"

"The artist's real name." Though she felt dreadful, Charley couldn't help smiling at the stunned silence that followed her request.

"Are you kidding!" Dani exclaimed in a near shout.

"No."

"I will personally see to it," she promised excitedly. "But, Charley, why? And why now, for this show?"

"I'm tired, Dani," Charley replied honestly. "And I've decided I'm too old to play games anymore."

"About time too." Dani's sigh betrayed a wealth of relief. "I can't imagine how you've kept up the pretense all these years."

"By running around in circles, of course." Charley laughed derisively. "It seems, though, that I've run into myself, and I'm not overly fond of what I've discovered."

"You must be tired," Dani murmured. "You're not making any sense."

"I am to me," Charley retorted, then changed the subject. "By the way, could you find room on the walls for one more canvas?"

"Will you have time to finish it?" The business side of Dani came to the fore, drawing a genuine smile from Charley.

"It is finished."

"I'll make room."

Charley spent several more minutes discussing the show with Dani, then she hung up, asking herself, what next? She decided she ought to give her father a call. But she jerked back, startled, when the phone rang just as she reached for it.

"It's later, and I feel lucky. What's your answer?" Brant demanded.

Suddenly unsure, Charley hesitated. Don't blow it, she told herself, this man is all the everything you'll ever find on this earth.

"Yes." A whisper. A sigh. A surrender.

"When?" he asked softly.

Tell him. She knew she must tell him the truth. Drawing a deep breath, Charley blurted, "Right after my show."

There was a long silence.

"Show?" Charley imagined she could see Brant's brows join over his hawkish nose. "What show?"

"The one I'm having at the Longlott Gallery." Charley closed her eyes.

"Charlott," Brant said with infinite patience. "The only thing coming up at Longlott's is a showing of Max Charles's work."

"Yes." Again Charley held her breath, waiting, waiting for the light to switch on inside Brant's mind. She imagined she could hear the click when it did.

"You . . . you . . ." he whispered on a strangled note. "You're Max Charles?"

"Yes." Charley bit down hard on her lip.

"You, damn it! I could throttle you!" His tone was still incredulous. "I think I *will* throttle you!" Brant's voice grew stronger. "Damn it, Charlott! You stood by, no, encouraged, me to make a fool of myself by evaluating your work!"

"Brant, no!" she protested. "I truly wanted to hear your opinion." Charley broke the long silence this time. "Does knowing who I am change things?"

"Were you hoping it would?" Brant gave her no time

to respond. "If you were," he went on, "forget it. We'll be married the day after your show." Brant paused, then added softly, "Agreed?"

"Agreed." Relief made her feel lightheaded for a moment. When the sensation passed, she ventured, "Are you angry about Max Charles, Brant?"

"No." His deep-throated laughter made her feel lightheaded all over again. "Strange, but I feel very proud. Are you going to have dinner with me tonight?" he added, startling her into alertness.

"If you insist." Charley sighed audibly, blinking away tears of pure gladness.

"Don't get cute, Charlott—Max," Brant warned. "I'll be by at seven, okay?"

"Yes, Brant."

Charley didn't even bother to replace the receiver after disconnecting, but immediately punched in Dani's number again.

"This last work is a seascape," she rattled after Dani had said hello. "It is not for sale."

"But, Char-ley," Dani protested. "I've had dozens of requests for a Charles seascape!"

"Maybe next time," Charley promised. "But not this one. Hang a Sold sign on it, Dani. That's an order. 'Bye."

Again Charley disconnected, then punched in another number. Her father answered.

"Where's Darlene?" Charley demanded at once, fearing her father had scared the woman off.

"Shopping. Why?"

"Oh . . . ah . . ." Charley laughed freely, happily, for the first time in days. "I was afraid you'd frightened her away."

"Your confidence in me is heartwarming," Stephen drawled. "Actually Darlene is shopping for a dress to be married in."

"You too!" Charley yelped.

"No. I don't think I'll be shopping for a dress to be married in," he said dryly.

Charley groaned. "Dad, I meant, are you getting married too?"

"What do you mean by 'too'?" Stephen asked with slow deliberation.

Charley wet her lips, drew a deep breath, and plunged in. "Dad, Brant has asked me to marry him. I said yes."

"Good for you," Stephen approved. "You two should make a spectacular pair. I can't wait to see the fireworks." He laughed delightedly, then asked, "When's the day?"

Laughing along with him, Charley answered, "The day after my show."

"He knows?"

"He knows."

"Good." Stephen chuckled again. "We could make it a double wedding and really give the social matrons something to chatter about."

Charley loved the idea almost as much as she loved him. "You're on," she whooped. "Give my love to Darlene."

As Charley counted the number of days until her show she grew more nervous, more tense, more impatient with everything and everybody around her. Brant, displaying a mild steadiness she would not have believed him capable of, spoke softly and trod warily while in her company—which was most of the time. Only once did he venture a taunt about her reaping the rewards of her own foolishness, and that was at dinner the night of the day he proposed to her.

"Why did you ever begin this charade in the first place?" he demanded, still obviously put out. "Being Max Charles is certainly nothing to be ashamed of."

"I know that!" Charley had snapped, quaking at the mere thought of how he would react when he understood the extent of her foolishness. "I . . . had my reasons," she ended lamely.

"And now those reasons have begun to haunt you?" he taunted softly.

"Are you trying to drive me away from you?"

Brant had received her message loud and clear and had modeled himself after the perfect gentleman. He was seemingly content to escort Charley to dinner, to the theater, and, one Sunday afternoon, on a stroll in the park. He agreed readily to Stephen's suggestion of a double wedding, and charmed Darlene into constant praise of him.

But for Charley, the biggest surprise was Brant's control over his physical desire. Brant did not, by even the slightest overt move, pressure her. Every night he kissed her good night at the door to her apartment, turning away immediately after he lifted his mouth from hers. Charley might have worried that he'd lost interest if she had not witnessed the fire glowing in his dark eyes or heard the occasional sigh of frustration he let slip or felt the urgency in the hands that gripped her shoulders during those brief kisses.

Despite all her worry about the show, everything went perfectly. Charley, playing the rebellious beauty one last time, had the satisfaction of shocking her public on two counts. The first, of course, was her unveiling as Max Charles. The second came with the announcement of her and Brant's plan to marry the next day. The astounded expressions on the faces of the elite were wonderfully amusing. Even better was Brant's excitement on glimpsing the turbulent seascape, and his groan of disappointment on finding a Sold sticker on it. Charley derived extreme pleasure from informing Dani where to send the painting in three days' time.

Then it was over, everyone gone, almost every painting sold, and all Charley wanted was to take the final step in her plan. Tomorrow Brant would learn the complete truth about her. She both dreaded and eagerly anticipated the moment of revelation.

The morning of Charley's last day as a single person dawned bright and hot. Dull from lack of sleep and nervous from thinking about what awaited her within a few short hours, she sat at the kitchen table sipping a glass of grapefruit juice and listening morosely to the weather forecast on the radio. Accuweather was calling for the sunny morning to give way to a stormy afternoon.

"Tell me about it!" Charley muttered, rinsing her glass before returning to the bedroom to shower and dress.

It was to be a double wedding. She and Brant, along with Stephen and Darlene, would be married in the serene flower gardens at Louis's home. After the ceremony Louis would provide a wedding breakfast on the patio. Also, Louis and Gayle would stand as witnesses for both couples. There would be no other guests. Brant was to pick Charley up at eleven to drive them to his father's home.

When Charley opened her door to Brant at precisely eleven o'clock, the sight of him caused a thickening sensation in her throat and a tingling shiver along her spine. It was the night of her father's award dinner all over again.

Brant wore an expertly tailored, summerweight dark blue suit, a pristine white shirt that contrasted startlingly with his copper-colored skin, and a diagonally striped red and gray silk tie. He looked much too good for Charley's own welfare!

Brant returned her careful scrutiny, and the searching glance he gave her took her breath away. She had chosen to be married in an ivory suit and a sheer blouse in a shade of blue that matched her eyes. Her accessories were a deeper shade of blue.

"A mite too thin or not," he finally said softly, "you are one beautiful woman, Charlott."

"You're not half bad yourself," she quipped, laughing as he scowled down at her. "And I do thank you for the compliment."

"No compliment," Brant murmured, holding her arm as they walked to the elevator. "Simple fact. You project a very attractive image to the world."

Ensconced inside his big car, Charley replayed Brant's words over and over again in her mind, examining them for a hidden meaning. In an oblique way, had Brant been trying to tell her that what was behind the image was not nearly as attractive? Angry and upset at the same time, Charley remained unusually quiet throughout the drive to Louis's home. By the time they arrived she felt like one mass of tightly knotted nerves.

Everything went off as planned. Stephen looked handsome in light brown, Darlene lovely in soft apricot.

Louis, not surprisingly, was his aristocratic, urbane self, and Gayle was adorable in pastel pink.

The actual ceremony required all of eight minutes. The pastor gave his congratulations in one breath and his regrets for not being able to stay for brunch in the next. He had another wedding scheduled within the hour.

After the clergyman had made his departure and the others seated themselves around the glass-topped table on the patio, Charley excused herself to go to the powder room. She wanted to take some aspirin to calm the pounding that had begun in her right temple.

As Charley was returning to the patio she met Gayle in the dining room. Affixing a bright smile to her face, she quipped, "Next?"

Gayle returned her smile wanly. "I'm going to splash some cold water on my face," she explained. "It's getting more humid out there by the minute! Perhaps Louis should have planned the meal for indoors, where it's cool."

"Perhaps." A mischievous light sparkled in Charley's eyes. "Did I catch you and Louis holding hands several times at the show yesterday?"

Gayle's cheeks turned a becoming pink. "Yes," she admitted softly. "He's still protesting about the difference in our ages but, with Brant working on him from the inside, and me talking myself hoarse from my side, I think we're beginning to wear him down." She smiled dreamily. "Oh, Charley," she sighed. "He is so wonderful!"

I know the feeling, Charley thought, watching her friend sympathetically. Clasping Gayle's hand, she squeezed it encouragingly. "I'm sure he is, and as long as you feel so strongly about him, keep after him, don't let him get away.''

"The only place Louis is going to get to is the altar!" Gayle laughed, continuing on her way to the powder room.

Her composure firmly intact, Charley joined the party for brunch. Dreading the moment she and Brant would be alone together, she was hardly able to do justice to the sumptuous array of food. There was everything from poached oysters to roast beef and baked Virginia ham, with assorted side dishes between. She managed to taste some of the hot foods, but she consumed mostly fresh fruit and melon—and about a gallon of coffee!

Though Charley tarried at the table as long as she possibly could, the moment when she could procrastinate no longer eventually arrived. There was a general movement toward the cars, instigated by her new husband. After congratulations, hugs, kisses, and good-byes, Stephen and Darlene left to begin the long drive to their undisclosed getaway site in the Poconos, and Charley and Brant departed for his town house.

The drive back into the city was accomplished with little conversation, and what there was of it was rather stilted and banal.

"Are you disappointed at having to stay at the house instead of going away like your father and Darlene?" Brant asked after bringing the car to a stop inside the garage.

"No." At that particular moment she had much more important things than a wedding trip on her mind—like how her husband was going to react when he discovered she'd been deliberately misleading him all along! "I do understand the requirements of business, Brant,'' she said gently. ''If it's important for you to stay close to town at this time, then . . .'' Charley let her voice drift away.

''It is. There are several reasons for me to stay close to home, but the most important is a condo site we're working on.'' As they entered the house through the kitchen, he promised, ''Maybe we can get away for a few weeks in the fall.''

Murmuring a noncommittal response, Charley preceded him into the house. Brant went on to give her a detailed explanation of his need to remain in the city. It seemed that the high rise he was contracted to build was at a point in construction where he preferred to be on hand if needed. But despite that necessity he promised to give her as much of his undivided attention as possible during the first weeks of their marriage. His promise unsettled her more than the disappointment of an at-home honeymoon!

Charley went through the kitchen and stopped in the doorway of Brant's den, her gaze fastened on one of her paintings. Like the madonna that hung in Louis's library, this was one of the few works she had sold without knowing the identity of the purchaser. The painting was bold in its execution, the colors brilliant. The focal point of the canvas was the face of a man bathed in a glorious light. The man's hands were pictured with the palms out, as if he were pushing against some force. On the outer edge of the canvas were bright, jagged shards of glass that looked as though they had shattered moments before. But what immediately caught the eye of the viewer was the expression on the man's face. His features were alight with an almost shockingly intense pleasure. Charley had titled the work *Freedom;* it was her favorite of all.

"What type of freedom were you thinking of when you painted it?" Brant asked softly. He was standing so close behind her that Charley could feel his warm breath flutter her hair.

Though she hesitated, Charley answered with complete honesty. "Freedom from restrictions imposed by convention. Freedom of choice—*my* choice. Freedom to make my own decisions."

"Yes."

The simple confirmation confused Charley. Even without looking at him she knew he was staring at the painting. She just wasn't sure of exactly what he was seeing. Curious, yet at the same time not sure she wanted to know the answer, Charley let the subject drop.

"If you don't mind, I think I'll have a shower and a short nap." She slipped around him and walked back through the kitchen and along the hall to the stairs, where Brant brought her to a halt by placing his hand on her shoulder.

"Tired, hmmm?"

Fighting to keep the sudden feeling of excitement from showing on her face, Charley murmured, "Yes, and hot and sticky."

"It isn't hot in here." Leaning close to her, Brant brushed his face across her hair.

That's what *you* think! Charley compressed her lips. "No," she agreed. "The house is deliciously cool. But I'm still sticky." Moving away from him, she started up the stairs. "And the heat seems to have drained me of all energy. Did you . . . ah . . . have something in mind for this afternoon?" Of all the idiotic remarks, she thought, deciding she deserved the sardonic smile he gave her. Charley knew there were any number of rejoinders Brant could have embarrassed her with. Fortunately for her, he refrained from making them.

"Go have your shower, Charlott," he said softly.

Charley liked Brant's bedroom. She sized it up with her artistic eye and decided it made a bold statement of his masculinity. She padded around the room, stripping the damp clothes from her body and taking her lightest robe into the shower with her. The bathroom was equally masculine, and equally appreciated by Charley.

The cool spray beating against her hot skin was heavenly. After washing her face and brushing her teeth, Charley walked into the bedroom, desiring nothing more than to slip between cool sheets and sleep for several hours. She had taken three steps into the room when, lifting her eyes, she stopped dead, her gaze tangling with that of the tall man standing at the far window.

Brant had also obviously showered. His suit had been exchanged for a short terry robe and his hair was still damp. Brant looked achingly handsome and fiercely proud, and granite hard in his determination. Behind him the window revealed a sky that was rapidly darkening with clouds.

"The storm's moving in fast." He offered the weather report as he strolled to where she still stood, apparently rooted to the floor. "Looks like things are going to get a little wild for a while."

There was not the slightest nuance to betray a double meaning to his observation, yet Charley stiffened with a mixture of trepidation and anticipation. "Yes, well . . . I . . . ah . . . I always have liked sleeping with the sound of rain hitting the window," she babbled. Brant came to a stop just inches in front of her and Charley's heart began to beat wildly at his proximity.

"Really?" Brant lifted one hand to gently capture hers. "Odd," he continued, drawing her with him to the bed. "I can think of a much more interesting way to pass the time during a storm." Sitting on the edge of the bed, Brant urged her closer by placing both hands securely on her waist. "A pastime more in tune with the . . . elements, shall we say?" By the simple method of applying light pressure, he lowered her to her knees between his thighs. "Perfectly fitting," he went on in an intoxicating tone. And then, leaning toward her, he touched his lips to the corner of her mouth.

As had happened before and, she was now positive, would always happen when Brant touched her, Charley's rational mind ceased to function. Closing her eyes to savor the texture of his tongue as he glided it along her lower lip, she urged herself to tell Brant the truth before it was too late.

The next instant it was too late! Tightening his grip on her waist, Brant straightened, drawing her with him. The minute he was on his feet he swept her into his arms, only to put her down again—in the center of the wide bed. Bending over her, he untied the sash to her robe then delicately separated the material, exposing her flushed and shivering body to his passion-clouded eyes.

"You are even more beautiful than I imagined, and my imagination has been driving me up the wall!" Stretching his length out beside her, Brant caressed her cheek with his fingertips. "Satin," he pronounced in a whisper. His fingers trailed down her face to her throat, quickening every tiny nerve ending along the way. "I've met your price, Charlott. You are wearing the ring you demanded.'' His fingers trailed lower, outlining the swell at the side of her breast. ''You will not sleep through the storm.''

''Brant . . .'' Charley felt as if he had struck her a blow to the chest. She wanted to scream a protest, a denial, an objection, to the gently voiced insult he was punishing her with. She wanted to but could not.

Reason fled completely before the onslaught of Brant's caressing hands. Charley could not tell him the truth now; she could not tell him anything, for she was reduced to speechless appreciation of the new and wonderful sensations he was introducing her to.

Murmuring his name over and over, Charley drank as deeply from him as he did from her. Following the dictates of instinct, she caressed his body as freely, as wantonly, as he did hers. Glorying in the heady power she discovered she had over him, she submitted to the power he had over her.

In a barely audible tone Brant whispered darkly exciting love words, old as time, as new as tomorrow. When Charley could stand the tension coiling inside her no longer, she clung to him, begging for the fulfillment only he could grant her.

''Brant, please, please, please . . .''

The weight of his body was a joy to bear. When Brant hesitated at the first sign of resistance from her body, Charley was too caught up in the moment to realize why. Grasping his hips, she urged him on.

''Brant, don't tease! Not now!''

Brant murmured something she could not understand, then moved again only to go completely still when he met with resistance a second time. Bracing his body with his hands, he pushed himself up enough to stare into her face. A flicker of unreadable emotion crossed his features.

"The first time?" Brant's rough voice held disbelief and a strange note that sounded like awe. "Charlott!" His voice was still low, but stronger now. "This is your first time?"

"Yes." Charley's whisper was barely discernible. "I—I'm sorry, Brant."

"Sorry? Sorry!" He looked like he might laugh, but didn't. "My sweet, skinny Charley! The only thing to be sorry about is that I almost hurt you . . . needlessly!" Lowering his body to hers, he kissed her deeply. "I will be as gentle as possible, darling."

Consumed with the need to be one with him, euphoric at the sound of his endearment, Charley felt a mere moment's twinge of pain. Then all pain, all thought, fled before the desperate pleasure they gave to each other.

After the pleasure was over she knew the sweet joy of lying safe in Brant's arms as the storm made its way to the east and the ocean. Curled against his side, Charley turned her face into the curve of his neck and placed her parted lips on his skin, a rich taste indeed!

His arms tightened to draw her still closer, and Brant kissed the top of her head. "You are not only beautiful," he said deeply. "You are perfect."

With praise such as that, Charley mused drowsily, a woman could nap very soundly.

Charley had three delightful days of laughing, loving, and simply being with her husband. The phone broke their idyll on the fourth morning. Still at the breakfast table, Brant reached out for the phone.

"There's a problem at the site," he told her after he'd

finished the call. "Horning, my foreman, thinks it needs my attention." He rose from the table and bent to kiss her lingeringly. When he straightened he drew a long breath. "I sure hope this won't take all day."

He was gone within minutes. Dressed in dark green work pants and shirt and high, laced boots, he looked devastatingly attractive. After he left Charley moped around the house, straightening up, getting to know her new home, and generally trying to occupy herself. She was already growing restless, when the phone rang a second time.

"Charley! I'm sorry if I'm interrupting anything," Gayle began, "but I'm calling to invite you and my co-conspirator to dinner with us tonight!"

"Us?" Charley asked.

"Louis has surrendered! At least partly so. He has told me we'll have a trial engagement . . . just to see how it goes, mind you!" She giggled. "Will you come?"

"I'll have to ask Brant." Charley laughed with her friend, then went on to explain why she could not ask him at once. Promising to get back to Gayle with an answer as soon as possible, Charley hung up.

She was about to phone the construction site when she realized that Brant had left in such a hurry, neither one of them had thought about the possibility of his being needed at the site through the lunch hour. She could pack him a bag lunch and take it to him. The excitement that bubbled through her as she prepared sandwiches brought Charley to a full stop. Brant had left the house less than two hours ago yet here she was practically running around in circles at the idea of seeing him again.

Vulnerability! Not since she was seventeen had she

experienced such a feeling of vulnerability. And she found it both frightening and exhilarating to be at the mercy of another person that way. More than anything she wanted to be with Brant.

Decked out like a summer flower in a sheer cotton dress of deep apricot and palest peach, Charley arrived at the site some thirty-five minutes later. After parking her racy-looking car beside the black Cadillac, she picked her way carefully over the uneven terrain. With bright eyes she searched for the distinctive form of the man she'd irrevocably committed herself to.

As she neared the tall skeleton of the building under construction, her eyes unwillingly climbed the framework of the emerging tower. She shuddered in sympathy for the men working on that pile of steel. Her gaze had inched its way to the seventh level, when all the breath rushed from her body with an audible *whoosh*. There was a man striding confidently along an outside beam. He was taller than most, with dark hair visible beneath the hard hat he was wearing, and copper-colored skin gleaming in the midday sunlight. The man was dressed in dark green pants and shirt. The man was her husband!

Afraid to watch him stroll along the thin piece of steel, yet unable to tear her gaze away, Charley froze in place. She longed to cry out to him, beg him to come down to safety, but when she opened her mouth, the sound could not get past the dry thickness of her throat and lips.

First Charley's palms grew wet, then the earth seemed to undulate under her and her vision began to darken. Then she had the oddest sensation, like floating, drifting, free-falling in space.

"Brant!"

Checking his confident stride midway along the narrow steel beam, Brant glanced around at the worker who'd called his name. The man was pointing to the ground.

"A lady just fell over down there!"

Without fear of his precarious position, Brant swung around to scan the ground. His heart seemed to jolt to a stop at the sight of Charlott's mass of dark red hair fanned out on the yellowish earth.

"Charlott!" Her name was torn from his throat as he fairly leaped the remaining yards to the open lift. What was she doing on the site? What was wrong? Why was she lying on the ground? Had she tripped on the uneven terrain? Had she suffered sunstroke? God! Was she all right? The thoughts skipped through Brant's mind as he rode the elevator to the ground, then all conjecturing ceased as he took off at a dead run. He pushed the curious men out of his way and made a mad dash for the woman he now knew he loved more than anyone else on earth.

What the devil? Charley opened her eyes, then blinked against the harshness of the bright sunlight. What had happened to her? she wondered, lifting an oddly weak arm to touch her hand to her forehead. She felt so very hot, yet her skin felt strangely cold!

"Are you all right, miss?"

Blinking again, Charley focused her gaze on the man who'd anxiously asked the question. He was kneeling beside her, his black face sheened with sweat, his expression revealing frightened concern. Charley tried to smile and attempted to sit up.

"I—I think so." Her smile wobbled. "How extraordinary! Did I faint?"

"Must have." The man slid his arm around her shoulders to steady her. "I saw you go down; you just seemed to crumple up."—an encouraging grin split his watchful face—"like an accordion." His hand tightened on her upper arm, stopping her when she tried to stand up. "I think you'd better give it a minute, lady."

"No, really, I'm fine now," Charley insisted, suffering more now from embarrassment than anything else. "I feel so fooli—"

"Charlott! What the hell!" Brant's voice cut across hers as he dropped to his knees on the other side of her. "Are you sick?"

"Oh, Brant!" Unconcerned with the curious eyes of the dozen or so men standing around, Charley flung her arms around Brant's neck. "I'm sorry! I've never fainted before in my life!"

"Too much sun, Brant?" The man on the other side of her queried as he relinquished his grasp on her arm.

"Hell, I don't know!" Scooping her into his arms, Brant stood up, bearing her weight with effortless ease. "For all I know she could be pregnant!"

"Oh, Brant, for heaven's sake!" Angling her head to face the other man, Charley hurried to explain. "It's much too soon for speculation of that kind." Obviously her explanation was none too clear, for the man shot a frown at Brant.

"My wife, Charlott," Brant supplied. "Charlott, this is my foreman, Rafe Horning."

"Glad to meet you, Mrs. d'Acier." Rafe favored Charley with a blindingly white smile. "Even though I would have preferred to be introduced under more pleasant conditions." Reaching out, he grasped the hand Charley extended. "I hope you'll be very happy with this nutty half-breed.'' The scowl Brant threw him merely widened his smile.

"I . . . thank you, Rafe, I—''

"I'm taking Charlott home, Rafe,'' Brant interrupted. "If you should need me again . . .''

"No, I think we've got everything under control now. Sorry I had to call you out here.''

Brant carried her to his Cadillac, set her on her feet while he unlocked it, and rattled off instructions about having her car delivered to the house. Then he was swinging the door open and telling her to sit down.

"I'm taking you to see a doctor,'' Brant said as he drove off the site.

"No! Brant, I'm fine now, truly!'' Sliding down on the seat, Charley rested her head against the back and closed her eyes. "I just need to rest for a little while.''

Though Brant's lips set into a thin, straight line, he didn't argue. Sighing with relief, Charley kept her eyes closed, and her mouth shut throughout the twenty-minute drive home.

When they arrived at the town house, Brant carried her inside and up the stairs to the bedroom. "I still think you should see a doctor,'' he muttered as he settled her on top of the bedspread she'd neatly smoothed that morning. Sitting on the bed beside her, Brant imprisoned her by placing his hands on either side of her arms. Bending over her, he stared at her with worry in his eyes. "What happened out there, Charlott?''

"I . . .'' She shrugged. "I fainted.''

"Damn it! People do not faint without reason!'' Brant's features tautened with strain. "You seem perfectly healthy but . . .''

"I *am* perfectly healthy!'' Feeling foolish now that the

incident was over, and afraid of revealing the true extent of her feelings by telling him the truth, Charley raked her mind for a plausible explanation.

"Then what caused it?" Brant pleaded. "Charlott, if I thought my insistence on marriage put you under stress, I'd . . ." Brant paused to swallow, yet when he continued, his voice had a dry, raspy sound. "These last few days have been so very good for me, I guess I assumed they were good for you too."

"They were! Brant, do you think I'd have explained all my feelings to you if I weren't happy about the marriage?" Although there was still much she and Brant did not know about each other, they had had long discussions during the previous three days, and many of the gaps had been filled in. Charley now knew that Brant was everything her father had claimed he was, and then some. Brant was now cognizant of the double life she'd been living, and her reasons, however misguided, for it. The one thing they had not exchanged were vows of love. Perhaps the best course would be to continue her revelations and tell him the real cause of her fainting. "I was scared," she blurted out starkly.

"Scared?" Brant repeated blankly. "Scared of what?"

"Seeing you up there." Charley shifted her eyes and her gaze was caught by the painting that had been delivered less than a half hour before she'd left the house to go to the construction site. "Actually," she went on in a whisper, "I was terrified. I wanted to scream at you to come down from there."

"But why?" Brant's tone conveyed confusion.

"I could see you, in my mind's eye, falling, striking the ground. . . . Brant! I suffer from acute acrophobia and vertigo! Observing *any*body positioned up high makes me feel ill. Seeing *you* up there . . ." Charley bit her lip to contain the shudder that tore through her body.

Brant lowered his body to hers and his weight was comforting, the sound of his voice was caressing. "Darling, don't think about it." Catching her chin with his fingers, he turned her face to his. "You shouldn't have come out to the site with those kinds of phobias." He made no attempt to conceal the relief that washed his features or the teasing light that sprang to his eyes. "You didn't think I was building a long house out there, did you?"

"Oh, Brant!" Charley buried her face in the curve of his neck to muffle her laughter. Luxuriating in the strength of his body, she slid her arms around his waist. Suddenly he went rigidly still. "Brant, what is it?" she asked softly.

"The seascape." Brant's tone was quizzical. "Charlott, that's your seascape on the wall! The one that was marked sold at the show."

Reluctantly raising her head, Charley glanced at the painting, which rested against the wall nearest his side of the bed. "Yes, I know. I had asked Dani to mark it sold. It was delivered after you left this morning. It's my wedding gift to you." Although Charley spoke her last sentence with apparent calm, she held her breath as she waited for his reaction. She didn't have to wait long.

"It was mine all the time? Even when I was trying to buy it?" He laughed down at her.

"Yes." Charley nodded solemnly. "Just like I was. You never had to buy me, darling."

"You mean you loved me all along? Is that why you were so terrified out at the site?"

"Yes," Charley murmured, then, her voice strong with her own conviction, "Yes, I love you. More than anything or anybody else."

"Ah, Charlott." Brant kissed her softly, tenderly. When he lifted his head to gaze at her, it was with eyes glowing with an exciting combination of deep love and rampant desire. "You see how it is with us?" Brant's lips twitched in amusement as he repeated the words he'd said to her after their day in the sun. "God! I love you! I hope it is always this way with us." Capturing her mouth with his, Brant proceeded to show her exactly how it was.

Sliding her arms down his chest, Charley put her trembling fingers to work on the buttons of his shirt, longing, needing, to know the feel of him against her palms. When the necessity for breath parted their mouths, she pressed her lips to the base of his throat, finding the flavor of him both sweet and salty. Extending the tip of her tongue, she licked his skin, delighting in the responsive shudder that rippled the length of his body.

"What are you doing?" Brant murmured thickly into her hair. "I'm dusty and sweaty from the site!"

Charley laughed softly and wriggled more closely to his inviting hardness.

"I did warn you about my taste for rich things, darling," she teased. "And you are definitely the richest thing I've ever tasted in my life."

*Fall in love again for the first time
every time you read a Silhouette Romance novel.*

If you enjoyed this book, and you're ready to be carried away by more tender romance...get 4 romance novels FREE when you become a Silhouette Romance home subscriber.

Act now and we'll send you four touching Silhouette Romance novels. They're our gift to introduce you to our convenient home subscription service. Every month, we'll send you six new Silhouette Romance books. Look them over for 15 days. If you keep them, pay just $11.70 for all six. Or return them at no charge.

We'll mail your books to you two full months *before they are available anywhere else.* Plus, with every shipment, you'll receive the Silhouette Books Newsletter absolutely free. *And Silhouette Romance is delivered free.*

Mail the coupon today to get your four free books—and more romance than you ever bargained for.

Silhouette Romance is a service mark and a registered trademark
of Simon & Schuster, Inc.

IT'S YOUR OWN SPECIAL TIME

Contemporary romances for today's women.
Each month, six very special love stories will be yours
from SILHOUETTE.

$1.75 each

☐ 104 Vitek	☐ 131 Stanford	☐ 159 Tracy	☐ 186 Howard
☐ 105 Eden	☐ 132 Wisdom	☐ 160 Hampson	☐ 187 Scott
☐ 106 Dailey	☐ 133 Rowe	☐ 161 Trent	☐ 188 Cork
☐ 107 Bright	☐ 134 Charles	☐ 162 Ashby	☐ 189 Stephens
☐ 108 Hampson	☐ 135 Logan	☐ 163 Roberts	☐ 190 Hampson
☐ 109 Vernon	☐ 136 Hampson	☐ 164 Browning	☐ 191 Browning
☐ 110 Trent	☐ 137 Hunter	☐ 165 Young	☐ 192 John
☐ 111 South	☐ 138 Wilson	☐ 166 Wisdom	☐ 193 Trent
☐ 112 Stanford	☐ 139 Vitek	☐ 167 Hunter	☐ 194 Barry
☐ 113 Browning	☐ 140 Erskine	☐ 168 Carr	☐ 195 Dailey
☐ 114 Michaels	☐ 142 Browning	☐ 169 Scott	☐ 196 Hampson
☐ 115 John	☐ 143 Roberts	☐ 170 Ripy	☐ 197 Summers
☐ 116 Lindley	☐ 144 Goforth	☐ 171 Hill	☐ 198 Hunter
☐ 117 Scott	☐ 145 Hope	☐ 172 Browning	☐ 199 Roberts
☐ 118 Dailey	☐ 146 Michaels	☐ 173 Camp	☐ 200 Lloyd
☐ 119 Hampson	☐ 147 Hampson	☐ 174 Sinclair	☐ 201 Starr
☐ 120 Carroll	☐ 148 Cork	☐ 175 Jarrett	☐ 202 Hampson
☐ 121 Langan	☐ 149 Saunders	☐ 176 Vitek	☐ 203 Browning
☐ 122 Scofield	☐ 150 Major	☐ 177 Dailey	☐ 204 Carroll
☐ 123 Sinclair	☐ 151 Hampson	☐ 178 Hampson	☐ 205 Maxam
☐ 124 Beckman	☐ 152 Halston	☐ 179 Beckman	☐ 206 Manning
☐ 125 Bright	☐ 153 Dailey	☐ 180 Roberts	☐ 207 Windham
☐ 126 St. George	☐ 154 Beckman	☐ 181 Terrill	☐ 208 Halston
☐ 127 Roberts	☐ 155 Hampson	☐ 182 Clay	☐ 209 LaDame
☐ 128 Hampson	☐ 156 Sawyer	☐ 183 Stanley	☐ 210 Eden
☐ 129 Converse	☐ 157 Vitek	☐ 184 Hardy	☐ 211 Walters
☐ 130 Hardy	☐ 158 Reynolds	☐ 185 Hampson	☐ 212 Young

$1.95 each

☐ 213 Dailey	☐ 219 Cork	☐ 225 St. George	☐ 231 Dailey
☐ 214 Hampson	☐ 220 Hampson	☐ 226 Hampson	☐ 232 Hampson
☐ 215 Roberts	☐ 221 Browning	☐ 227 Beckman	☐ 233 Vernon
☐ 216 Saunders	☐ 222 Carroll	☐ 228 King	☐ 234 Smith
☐ 217 Vitek	☐ 223 Summers	☐ 229 Thornton	☐ 235 James
☐ 218 Hunter	☐ 224 Langan	☐ 230 Stevens	☐ 236 Maxam

Silhouette Romance

$1.95 each

- ☐ 237 Wilson
- ☐ 238 Cork
- ☐ 239 McKay
- ☐ 240 Hunter
- ☐ 241 Wisdom
- ☐ 242 Brooke
- ☐ 243 Saunders
- ☐ 244 Sinclair
- ☐ 245 Trent
- ☐ 246 Carroll
- ☐ 247 Halldorson
- ☐ 248 St. George
- ☐ 249 Scofield
- ☐ 250 Hampson
- ☐ 251 Wilson
- ☐ 252 Roberts
- ☐ 253 James
- ☐ 254 Palmer
- ☐ 255 Smith
- ☐ 256 Hampson
- ☐ 257 Hunter
- ☐ 258 Ashby
- ☐ 259 English
- ☐ 260 Martin
- ☐ 261 Saunders
- ☐ 262 John

- ☐ 263 Wilson
- ☐ 264 Vine
- ☐ 265 Adams
- ☐ 266 Trent
- ☐ 267 Chase
- ☐ 268 Hunter
- ☐ 269 Smith
- ☐ 270 Camp
- ☐ 271 Allison
- ☐ 272 Forrest
- ☐ 273 Beckman
- ☐ 274 Roberts
- ☐ 275 Browning
- ☐ 276 Vernon
- ☐ 277 Wilson
- ☐ 278 Hunter
- ☐ 279 Ashby
- ☐ 280 Roberts
- ☐ 281 Lovan
- ☐ 282 Halldorson
- ☐ 283 Payne
- ☐ 284 Young
- ☐ 285 Gray
- ☐ 286 Cork
- ☐ 287 Joyce
- ☐ 288 Smith

- ☐ 289 Saunders
- ☐ 290 Hunter
- ☐ 291 McKay
- ☐ 292 Browning
- ☐ 293 Morgan
- ☐ 294 Cockcroft
- ☐ 295 Vernon
- ☐ 296 Paige
- ☐ 297 Young
- ☐ 298 Hunter
- ☐ 299 Roberts
- ☐ 300 Stephens
- ☐ 301 Palmer
- ☐ 302 Smith
- ☐ 303 Langan
- ☐ 304 Cork
- ☐ 305 Browning
- ☐ 306 Gordon
- ☐ 307 Wildman
- ☐ 308 Young
- ☐ 309 Hardy
- ☐ 310 Hunter
- ☐ 311 Gray
- ☐ 312 Vernon
- ☐ 313 Rainville
- ☐ 314 Palmer

- ☐ 315 Smith
- ☐ 316 Macomber
- ☐ 317 Langan
- ☐ 318 Herrington
- ☐ 319 Lloyd
- ☐ 320 Brooke
- ☐ 321 Glenn
- ☐ 322 Hunter
- ☐ 323 Browning
- ☐ 324 Maxam
- ☐ 325 Smith
- ☐ 326 Lovan
- ☐ 327 James
- ☐ 328 Palmer
- ☐ 329 Broadrick
- ☐ 330 Ferrell
- ☐ 331 Michaels
- ☐ 332 McCarty
- ☐ 333 Page
- ☐ 334 Hohl
- ☐ 335 Bishop
- ☐ 336 Young
- ☐ 337 Sands
- ☐ 338 Gray
- ☐ 339 Morland

Silhouette **Romance**

Coming Next Month

SOLDIER OF FORTUNE
by Diana Palmer

•

PROMISE ME FOREVER
by Debbie Macomber

•

RISK FACTOR
by Naomi Horton

•

TENDER TAKEOVER
by Joan Smith

•

LOVING DECEPTION
by Lori Herter

•

CATCH A RISING STAR
by Tracy Sinclair